Erle Stanley Gardner and The Murder Room

>>> This title is part of The Murder Room, our series dedicated to making available out-of-print or hard-to-find titles by classic crime writers.

Crime fiction has always held up a mirror to society. The Victorians were fascinated by sensational murder and the emerging science of detection; now we are obsessed with the forensic detail of violent death. And no other genre has so captivated and enthralled readers.

Vast troves of classic crime writing have for a long time been unavailable to all but the most dedicated frequenters of second-hand bookshops. The advent of digital publishing means that we are now able to bring you the backlists of a huge range of titles by classic and contemporary crime writers, some of which have been out of print for decades.

From the genteel amateur private eyes of the Golden Age and the femmes fatales of pulp fiction, to the morally ambiguous hard-boiled detectives of mid twentieth-century America and their descendants who walk our twenty-first century streets, The Murder Room has it all. >>>

The Murder Room
Where Criminal Minds Meet

themurderroom.com

T0352220

Erle Stanley Gardner (1889–1970)

Born in Malden, Massachusetts, Erle Stanley Gardner left school in 1909 and attended Valparaiso University School of Law in Indiana for just one month before he was suspended for focusing more on his hobby of boxing that his academic studies. Soon after, he settled in California, where he taught himself the law and passed the state bar exam in 1911. The practise of law never held much interest for him, however, apart from as it pertained to trial strategy, and in his spare time he began to write for the pulp magazines that gave Dashiell Hammett and Raymond Chandler their start. Not long after the publication of his first novel, *The Case of the Velvet Claws*, featuring Perry Mason, he gave up his legal practice to write full time. He had one daughter, Grace, with his first wife, Natalie, from whom he later separated. In 1968 Gardner married his long-term secretary, Agnes Jean Bethell, whom he professed to be the real 'Della Street', Perry Mason's sole (although unacknowledged) love interest. He was one of the most successful authors of all time and at the time of his death, in Temecula, California in 1970, is said to have had 135 million copies of his books in print in America alone.

By Erle Stanley Gardner
(titles below include only those
published in the Murder Room)

Perry Mason series

The Case of the Sulky Girl
  (1933)
The Case of the Baited Hook
  (1940)
The Case of the Borrowed
  Brunette (1946)
The Case of the Lonely
  Heiress (1948)
The Case of the Negligent
  Nymph (1950)
The Case of the Moth-Eaten
  Mink (1952)
The Case of the Glamorous
  Ghost (1955)
The Case of the Terrified
  Typist (1956)
The Case of the Gilded Lily
  (1956)
The Case of the Lucky Loser
  (1957)
The Case of the Long-Legged
  Models (1958)
The Case of the Deadly Toy
  (1959)
The Case of the Singing Skirt
  (1959)
The Case of the Duplicate
  Daughter (1960)
The Case of the Blonde
  Bonanza (1962)

Cool and Lam series

The Bigger They Come (1939)
Turn on the Heat (1940)
Gold Comes in Bricks (1940)
Spill the Jackpot (1941)
Double or Quits (1941)
Owls Don't Blink (1942)
Bats Fly at Dusk (1942)
Cats Prowl at Night (1943)
Crows Can't Count (1946)
Fools Die on Friday (1947)
Bedrooms Have Windows
  (1949)
Some Women Won't Wait (1953)
Beware the Curves (1956)
You Can Die Laughing (1957)
Some Slips Don't Show (1957)
The Count of Nine (1958)
Pass the Gravy (1959)
Kept Women Can't Quit (1960)
Bachelors Get Lonely (1961)
Shills Can't Count Chips (1961)

Try Anything Once (1962)
Fish or Cut Bait (1963)
Up For Grabs (1964)
Cut Thin to Win (1965)
Widows Wear Weeds (1966)
Traps Need Fresh Bait (1967)

Doug Selby D.A. series

The D.A. Calls it Murder (1937)
The D.A. Holds a Candle (1938)
The D.A. Draws a Circle (1939)
The D.A. Goes to Trial (1940)
The D.A. Cooks a Goose (1942)
The D.A. Calls a Turn (1944)
The D.A. Takes a Chance (1946)
The D.A. Breaks an Egg (1949)

Terry Clane series

Murder Up My Sleeve (1937)
The Case of the Backward
  Mule (1946)

Gramp Wiggins series

The Case of the Turning Tide
  (1941)
The Case of the Smoking
  Chimney (1943)

Two Clues (two novellas) (1947)

The D.A. Holds a Candle

Erle Stanley Gardner

An Orion book

Copyright © The Erle Stanley Gardner Trust 1938

This edition published by
The Orion Publishing Group Ltd
Orion House
5 Upper St Martin's Lane
London WC2H 9EA

An Hachette UK company
A CIP catalogue record for this book is available from the British Library

ISBN 978 1 4719 0934 4

www.orionbooks.co.uk

CAST OF CHARACTERS

CAST OF CHARACTERS

CAST OF CHARACTERS

CHAPTER I

WEAK rays from a jaundiced sun penetrated the curtain of smudge smoke which hung over Madison City. Despite the fact that it was nine o'clock in the morning, the thermometer hung close to freezing.

It was a period of war, during which harassed citrus growers marshaled every possible defense to repel the invasion of the frost king. A peculiar combination of atmospheric conditions had brought a body of cold air sliding down from the snow-capped mountains in the far interior, across the plateau of desert, to drop in an icy blast upon the fertile citrus lands of the California coastline.

It was the third day of the frost blight. Ranchers had thrown up a defense smudge smoke which lay as a black pall over the community. During the cold mornings this smudge smoke hung thickly over the valley, dispersing in the chill afternoons, while sleepless ranchers, with red-rimmed eyes, frantically strove to get enough fuel to keep their smudge pots going for another night.

Since Madison City was an agricultural community, and since the businessmen realized all too well the stark ruin which awaited them during periods of farming disaster, they put up with the inconvenience of soot-bearing smudge smoke, spending disconsolate hours in storerooms which were inadequately heated. Residents huddled in houses which had been designed for a frostless climate, attempting to keep rooms livable with various types of gas heaters. Nostrils blackened by smudge smoke, they shivered through the cold spell, deriving only scant comfort from the knowledge that, like all freakish weather, it could not last much longer.

Doug Selby, tall, young, filled with the vigor of enthusiasm, walked rapidly down the second floor corridor of Madison City's courthouse. He latchkeyed the door marked "DISTRICT ATTORNEY—*Private*," hung up his overcoat, and pressed the button which informed his secretary he had arrived. There was steam heat in the courthouse, and Selby stood with his back to the radiator, enjoying the warmth. His secretary opened the door with a pile of mail, and smiled a greeting. Lights were on in the outer office, and Selby, with a discouraged glance at the vista of sooty half darkness which lay beyond the window, reached across to click on his own light switch. "What's in the mail," he asked; "anything important?"

"Nothing pressing," she said. "Ross Blaine is waiting."

"Blaine?" Selby repeated the name as he puckered his forehead in an effort at recollection.

"The young man who forged the check on the Madison City Transfer & Storage Company," she reminded him.

"Oh, yes," Selby said. He picked up the desk telephone and said to the operator, "See if Rex Brandon's in, will you?" and, a minute later, when he heard the sheriff's voice on the telephone, said, "This is Doug Selby talking, Rex. You'll remember I spoke to you about young Blaine who forged a check on the transfer company? Because of Blaine's mother, neither the restaurant that cashed the check nor the transfer company wants to prosecute, but Blaine doesn't know that yet. He's in my office and it may be a talk with him will do the boy some good."

"Coming right in," Brandon said.

"Okay, Rex. I'll leave the door of the private office open for you." Selby hung up the telephone and said to his secretary, "When I press the buzzer you can send young Blaine in here." As his secretary returned to the outer office, Selby ran rapidly through the pile of mail. Then he moved over to the door of his private office to open it as he heard Rex Brandon's step in the corridor.

The sheriff was twenty-five years older than Selby. His hair was sprinkled with gray. His face had been tanned to the color of saddle leather, and his legs were bowed from years spent on horseback, but his step was alert and springy. He flashed Selby a smile from friendly gray eyes which could, on occasion, become as hard and cold as twin chunks of ice, and said, "Cold enough for you, Doug?"

"I'll say," Selby said. "I couldn't get enough covers last night." And, looking at the grime on his hands, "I think it'll be the Fourth of July before I can get clean."

Rex Brandon dropped into a chair, fished a cloth sack of tobacco and a package of brown cigarette papers from his pocket. "How do you figure this Blaine chap, Doug?"

Selby ran long, tapering fingers through his wavy hair. "How do *you* figure him, Rex?" he countered.

"In my day," the sheriff said, "kids who forged checks went to jail. Therefore, there weren't many kids who forged checks."

Selby's eyes shifted to look past the sheriff at the sooty window. "Times have changed a lot," he said, "and yet . . . well, Rex, we've gained something, and lost something."

Fatherly affection showed in the sheriff's eyes as he looked at the young district attorney. "When I was a kid, Doug, the young chaps were more earnest. They don't seem to have the ambition nowadays. They get what they want too easy. You're different. You're just a kid, after all, and yet you hit this town like a mad bull charging a rail fence. Gosh, you climbed into the political scrap, got swept into office . . . oh, shucks, why aren't more of these college critters like you?"

Selby laughed. "For one thing, there's only one district attorneyship in the county, Rex. All the young bloods couldn't go after that. But, no kidding, Rex, there aren't the opportunities now there were a few years ago. As people point out, there's plenty of room at the top; but you can't start climbing without first elbowing your way to the bottom of the ladder. I know something about young Blaine. His mother sacrificed a lot to give him a good education. But he can't use it, because he can't get a start. His education fitted him for a place at the top of the heap. It didn't show him how to scramble around at the bottom. Teaching a kid how to drive a high-powered automobile doesn't fit him to drive plow horses."

"Well, he could learn," Brandon said, shaking golden

3

grains of tobacco into a cupped paper. "That's what I had to do."

"Yes, but you learned when you were in your 'teens. These days, boys stay in school until they're . . . oh, well, Rex, let's get him in and see *why* he did it. I think that may make a difference. Blaine isn't a criminal, and I don't want to make him one. Let's see if we can't have a talk with him and get right down to brass tacks."

As Brandon nodded, rolling the cigarette into shape and drawing his tongue along the edge of the paper, Selby pressed the button which sounded a buzzer in the outer office. A moment later the door opened and a well-dressed young man of twenty-four entered, to stand staring at them, fighting to keep the panic from his eyes. "Sit down, Blaine," the district attorney said. When the young man had seated himself, Selby went on: "I suppose you know why you're here?" Blaine said nothing.

Selby opened the drawer of his desk, took out a check, and said, "Up to a couple of months ago, Blaine, you were employed as assistant bookkeeper at the Madison City Transfer & Storage Company. As bookkeeper, you had authority to sign checks up to three hundred dollars. Day before yesterday you cashed a check for sixty-five dollars at a local restaurant. That check was on a regular printed blank of the Madison City Transfer & Storage Company. The bank, however, had been advised that your employment had been terminated, and refused payment when the check was presented."

Blaine raised his eyes, glancing quickly at the district attorney, then averted them and nodded. After a moment, he gulped and said, "Yes, sir."

"Why did you do it?" Selby asked.

"I don't know," Blaine said.

"Now, that's no answer, Ross," Selby said, not unkindly. "You knew the bank would refuse to pay the check. You knew you were violating the law. You must have had some compelling reason for doing it."

"I needed the money," Blaine said.

"Why did you need the money?"

"I just needed it."

Selby stared steadily at the young man and went on: "I'm going to talk turkey to you, Ross. You have a widowed mother. She has a small annuity on which she can get by. But she can't support you on that annuity. *You* should be bringing in a little more money to add to the family income. You've held two jobs in the last year. You haven't lasted at either of them. I had a long talk with Charlie Peters at the Madison City Transfer & Storage Company. He says he had to let you go because you simply didn't take any interest in your job. He thought you were playing around so much nights that you were half dead from lack of sleep. Two or three times he caught you with a hangover. You looked at your work as a dull routine in which you hadn't the slightest interest. As a result, you made mistakes. You were just about as valuable as a piece of animated furniture. You could answer the telephone and mark down figures, but you couldn't put any life in your voice when you talked on the telephone and your figures didn't add up correctly. Once or twice a week the office had to overhaul everything in order to find why the figures didn't balance. It would be some careless mistake you'd made. So Peters let you go.

"Now, I'm going to tell you something else, Ross. At the time Peters let you go, you must have intended to forge this check. It's drawn on the First National on a check which was printed specially for the transfer company. You must have put that blank in your pocket, thinking that some time you'd use it and . . ."

Blaine blurted a denial. "I just happened to find that check in my wallet," he said.

"And how did it *happen* to get in your wallet?" the sheriff asked skeptically.

"I had some figures to write down," Blaine said, "and I didn't have any paper handy. They were figures that came in over the telephone. So I pulled this check out of the book and made a pencil note on the back of the check."

Selby regarded the back of the check, then nodded. "Yes," he said, "I can see where there were figures written here in pencil. Perhaps you're telling the truth, and this wasn't a deliberately planned crime. Now then, day before yesterday you needed money. What did you need it for?"

"I . . . Well, I had some debts to pay and I wanted the money."

Sheriff Brandon flashed Selby a significant glance. "Let me ask him a couple of questions, Doug," he said. Selby nodded, and Blaine turned his eyes reluctantly toward the sheriff. "I saw you riding with young George Stapleton the night before last," Brandon said. "You were in Stapleton's new car and headed out toward the Palm Thatch."

The boy was silent. Brandon waited a minute and said: "Stapleton's dad has money and can dish it out if he wants to. Since he's been in New York, George has been hitting the high spots. You went to school with George and you were on the football team with him. You're buddies. But you'd better tumble to the fact you can't keep up with Stapleton's pace."

Brandon ceased talking, and Blaine said nothing. "What were you doing out at the Palm Thatch?" Doug Selby asked.

"Just sitting around."

"Have something to drink?"

"Just some beer."

"Where did you go when you left there?"

"Home."

"What time did you leave?"

"About two o'clock."

Selby's eyes narrowed. "What time did you go out?"

"About ten."

"And you sat around there for four hours, drinking?"

"Oh, we were just killing time."

"Any girls there?" Selby asked.

Blaine shook his head. "Just the hostess. We were on a stag party."

Selby said, "How long has young Stapleton had his new car?"

"Two or three weeks."

"Didn't you drive around any to try it out?"

6

"No."

"Had you ridden in it before?"

"Yes."

"Why did he sell his old car?"

"I don't know. He was tired of it, I guess. He sold it for a song. Only got seven fifty for it."

"Who did he sell it to?"

"Tom Cuttings. He used to be in school with us. He's down at Mirande Mesa now. He happened to be up here, and George just up and sold him the bus."

"For seven hundred and fifty dollars?"

"Yes," Blaine said, his voice showing enthusiasm for the first time. "I wish I'd known George wanted to sell it at that price. It certainly is a swell bus, bright red, trimmed with white, convertible, side mounts, supercharger. . . . It's worth two thousand bucks of anybody's money just the way it stands."

"You'd like to have bought it, Ross?" Selby asked.

"I'll say I would . . . Why, that bus is . . . oh, well, what's the use? I couldn't have even bought the tail light. . . . But it's a swell job, she purrs along as easy . . ."

Selby interrupted him. "Can't you see what you're doing to yourself, Ross? When I talk to you about your mother and your duty to help support her, you don't show any enthusiasm, but when the talk shifts to an automobile which only a wealthy man should be driving, you're all ears. You won't face realities, you're living in a dream world. Snap out of it! Come down to earth. I started talking about that automobile because I knew just how you'd react. I wanted to show you to yourself."

The boy said sullenly, "Yes, sir."

"What did you boys do out at the Palm Thatch, Ross?"

"Nothing."

Rex Brandon said, "You played poker, didn't you, Ross?"

"Well, there was a little game running and we sat in on it."

"Who was playing?" Brandon asked.

"Oh, I don't like to snitch on anyone," Blaine said.

"Was Stapleton playing?"

7

"Ask him."

"How about the proprietor, Oscar Triggs? Did he know the game was going on?"

Blaine started to say something, then became silent.

Selby said, "I'm not trying to make you turn informer, Ross. I want to know what's going on out there because I don't want other young men to get caught in the same trap you did." Blaine sat silent, trying to avoid the young district attorney's eyes. "Come on, Ross," Selby said; "let's get it over with."

"You don't need to worry about anyone else getting caught in the same trap," Blaine said bitterly. "That trap was all set and baited for me."

"Why for you?"

Blaine raised tortured eyes. "Triggs wanted the skids under me because I'm in love with Madge Trent."

"Who's Madge Trent?"

"The hostess."

"I think," Selby said, his voice kindly, "that you'd better tell us some more about it, Ross."

Blaine clenched his hands, then started twisting his fingers. He looked up, his eyes glittering, and said, "All right. I'm no stool pigeon, but I'm not going to let Triggs frame me and take it on the chin without fighting back. You're right. There's a gambling game running out there three or four nights a week. There's a professional gambler comes up from Los Angeles whenever the big money turns up. He's after the big sucker, but sometimes he nicks Stapleton. Mostly, the gambler lays off us young fellows. If we can grab a few berries off the big money it's our cut for making things look on the level.

"But the other night Triggs knew I was down to brass tacks, and I think he figured I'd gone out on a limb for the dough I was putting in the game. He saw a good chance to put the skids under me. So he tipped off the professional, and they took me to the cleaners."

"Who's the gambler?" Selby asked.

"Carlo Handley."

"And the big money?"

"That's a retired broker by the name of Morley Need-

ham. He's a good scout, and he sure plays 'em
wide open. He don't care about losing his dough, just so he
has a good time. He likes to slip away from the city, come
up here and play around. Usually he brings a cutie with
him and buys a few stacks of chips for her. She takes the
winnings and he's sugar daddy for the losings. He's a fine
chap, an all around good scout. But this Handley has his
number. I think he has spotters hired to watch Needham.
Whenever Needham shows up, you can bank on it Handley will come rolling in, a half hour or so later, and then
the game really gets going.

"At first I used to drop out, but Handley winked at
me one night and said he didn't like too small a game,
and if I'd sit in he didn't think I'd lose my shirt—if I
kept it buttoned up. That was the start. I'd get a good
hand and nick Needham for a few dollars and Handley
would lay off. Sometimes Handley would even lose fifty
or sixty bucks to me. When Handley started raising, I'd
throw down my cards."

"How about young George Stapleton?"

"He can dish it out, and he can take it. I don't think
Handley *tries* to win from him, but he doesn't try not to.
He doesn't give George the breaks he does me. Needham's a wide open player. When he's lucky, he wins.
When he's unlucky, he loses his shirt. Handley knows
how to play him and always wins from him. Stapleton
doesn't. Sometimes Needham wins from Stapleton. I
think Stapleton's trying to play in too big time myself,
but that's not my business."

"And this hostess?" Selby asked.

Blaine's eyes softened. "She's on the up-and-up, as
square a shooter as you ever saw."

"What does she do?"

"In the game, you mean?"

"Yes."

"She doesn't play. She kids the trade along out front.
The games take place in back."

"Just how does she kid the trade along?" Sheriff Brandon asked.

Blaine flushed. His eyes angered, then shifted away

from the sheriff's. "She's a hostess," he said
surlily, "and that's all. She does a *hula* dance in a grass
skirt, and a barefoot temple dance. She shows a lot of
figure . . . and that's as far as she goes. She doesn't date.
Of course, the boys kid her along, and she comes and sits
at a table once in a while to keep things moving. She's a
good kid."

"Doesn't sound like much of a life for a decent girl,"
the sheriff said.

Blaine's eyes, smoldering with rage, flickered to the
sheriff's face, then dropped again. He made no comment,
but his lips were tight.

"What about Triggs?" Selby asked.

"Triggs is a smooth devil. He's nuts about Madge. He
puts the skids under anyone she looks at twice. That's
why he got me. He's a smooth, calm guy who never raises
a finger or a voice, but he sure gets what he goes after.
Right now he's after me . . . and I guess he's got me.

"He has almost a hypnotic influence over Madge. She
has to work, and a woman can't choose her work as easy
as some people think," with a sullen glance at the sheriff.
"In case you're blaming her, just remember she got married at eighteen and had a baby at nineteen. She's supporting that little girl now, and she can't make enough
money except by acting as hostess. But she makes 'em all
keep their distance. Only Triggs has her buffaloed. She
trembles every time he says something to her in that
deadly calm voice of his. I wish I had money enough to
take her out of that joint."

Selby put a hand on the boy's shoulder. "All right,
Ross. That's a good idea to have. Only you'll never get it
forging checks for stake-money in a poker game. You're
going to have to work, and work hard. Success still comes
through hard work. Sometimes a man flashes into the big
money like a skyrocket—but he usually comes right
down again—just a stick. Think you can remember
that?"

"Yes, Mr. Selby, I guess so. But I suppose I'm going
to have to go to jail. By the time I get out . . ."

"No, Ross, you're not going to jail. You're going home

and think things over. Then you're going to look for another job. And you're going to pay the sixty-five dollars back to the restaurant out of the first money you get. Do you understand?"

Blaine jumped to his feet, his face eager. "I'm not going to . . . I'm not arrested?"

"No," Selby said.

Blaine started for the door. His shoulders were squared as though a load had been lifted from them. In the doorway he turned. "Gee . . . thanks . . . thanks a lot!"

The door swung closed behind him. Selby walked to the closet and took out his overcoat. His face was set in lines of fighting determination. "I suppose," Rex Brandon said, grinning, "we're going out to see Triggs."

"We're going to see Triggs," Selby said. "Come on."

CHAPTER II

SMUDGE smoke still hung so low it was necessary for the sheriff to switch lights on the county car as they sped down the cold stretch of highway toward the city limits. "These road houses are a problem," the sheriff said. "They won't keep within the law on anything. And yet you hate to clamp the lid on so tight you spoil *all* the fun."

Selby stared at the flowing ribbon of cement. "We're going to make them quit running in professional gamblers," he said.

"It's next to impossible to get a conviction in a gambling case," Brandon pointed out. "Four or five of the lodge club rooms keep little gambling games running for the members, and people know that. Then there's a certain liberal element here that wants to see the county more wide open than it is. When Sam Roper was district attorney, things ran altogether too wide open. They say Roper was getting a slice of the graft. Things got so raw the voters swept us into office. We cleaned out all the joints and cut out all the graft. Now some of the people who voted for us are commencing to kick. They say we've sewed things up *too* tight.

"From all I can hear, this guy Triggs is a cool customer. Sam Roper is his lawyer. When Roper went back to private practice, he naturally started to represent all those places that . . ." Brandon suddenly slammed his foot on the brake. The car, which had been purring along at a smooth fifty miles an hour, slid sharply over to the right and slowed to a lurching stop.

"What is it?" Selby asked.

"That chap behind us," Brandon said.

Selby looked back through the window in the rear of the car, to where a man standing at the side of the road showed in distorted perspective because of the smoky atmosphere. The man slowly started toward them. "Just a hitch-hiker, Rex," the district attorney said. "He wants to go to Los Angeles. He'll be disappointed. He thinks we're stopping to give him a ride."

Brandon said, "I've seen that same chap hanging around on the road four or five times in the past ten days. He isn't any ordinary hitch-hiker. Let's find out what he wants."

The man came up to the car. "Going to Los Angeles?" he asked.

Brandon said, "Hop in, Buddy."

The man hesitated and said, "I have a partner down the road here three or four hundred yards. I wonder if you'll stop and pick him up too."

"Sure," Brandon said, winking at Selby, "we'll pick him up."

The man still hesitated. "He has a roll of blankets and a dog."

"Well, we're not taking any dogs," Selby said.

"All right, then," the hitch-hiker muttered. "I guess I can't take the lift."

Brandon pushed back the lapel of his coat. "This is the law," he said.

The man said, "Oh," in a flat, expressionless voice.

"What were you going to do in Los Angeles?" Brandon asked.

"Look for work."

"Know anyone there?"

"Yes. I have a couple of friends."

"What're their names?"

"Well, one of them's a Jim Smith and the other's a Frank Jones."

"Where do they live?"

"I don't know just where they live now. They're plumbers and I'd have to look around among the plumbers to find out where they are."

Brandon said, "You just moving on through?"

"Just moving on through," the man told him.

"From the East?"

"From the East."

"Where were you last night?"

"In Oceanside."

"And you came through this morning?"

"Yes. Got a ride through this far."

"First time you've ever been through here?"

"I was here once before about six months ago."

Brandon said, "All right. Now suppose you come clean. You've been hanging around this stretch of road for the last ten days. I've seen you four or five times. Who are you and what do you really want?" For a minute the man was silent. "Come on," Brandon said; "what's your name?"

"Emil Watkins."

"Where do you live, Watkins?"

The man appeared to be thinking for a minute. Suddenly he said, "All right. You've talked to me, now I'll talk to you. I'm not a crook. I know my rights. I've got enough dough so you can't vag me. If you want to see it, take a look." He pulled a wallet from his pocket, opened it, and pulled out a half dozen bills. "There's twenty dollars," he said, turning back one bill, "there's ten. There's five, and here are some ones. Now then, I'm minding my own business and that's all I ask anyone else to do."

Brandon slid from behind the steering wheel, walked around the car, his right hand held near the lapel of his coat. The hitch-hiker saw him coming, elevated his hands, holding his arms out away from his body. Sheriff Brandon patted him in search of a weapon, slid his hands along the man's body past his hips. "All right, Watkins," he said, turning back toward the car. "I just wanted to check up on you. Where do you live?"

"I'm traveling—looking for work. I'm sorry if I spoke out of turn, Sheriff. Honest, I'm headin' toward Los Angeles."

"Okay," the sheriff said, climbing back into the driver's seat. "You hadn't better be here when we get back, which'll be in about ten minutes. Just thought I'd check up on him," he explained to Doug Selby as he set the car into motion again. Three minutes later, the sheriff said, "Here's the Palm Thatch. Do you do the talking or do I?"

"I do," Selby said, as Brandon swung the wheel and guided the car into the gravel driveway of what had once been a pretentious country residence. The building had been remodeled and two long low wings added to each side. A neon sign bearing the words "PALM THATCH" surmounted the roof. The wings were roofed with palm leaves which had been nailed on above the shingles.

"Too early for anybody to be up now," Brandon said.

"There's smoke coming out of that chimney," Selby pointed out, as they parked the car in the circular gravel parking space and crossed to the door. Selby jabbed his thumb against the button and a few seconds later the door was opened by a short, bald-headed man in the late forties. He was freshly shaven, attired in a quiet gray business suit, and seemed self-effacing, all but his eyes. The eyes, cat-green and watchful, stared from beneath bushy blond eyebrows.

"Oscar Triggs?" Selby asked.

"Yes."

"I'm Douglas Selby, district attorney of the county. This is Rex Brandon, the sheriff."

Triggs said nothing, but continued to stand in the

doorway. "We're coming in," Selby said.

"Is this an official visit?" Triggs asked. "Because if it is, I want to telephone Mr. Roper, my lawyer. He'd want you to have a warrant."

Selby said, "You're running a place that's open to the public, Mr. Triggs, and we're coming in."

Triggs continued to stand in the doorway. Rex Brandon, with an impatient exclamation, pushed past Selby, shoved Triggs back against the wall and said, "Okay, Doug. Come on in."

Triggs recovered his balance, quietly closed the door behind them. He remained perfectly calm, a short-coupled, quiet man whose face showed no flicker of expression.

They entered a reception hallway in which stood an old-fashioned hat rack and umbrella stand. Back of the reception hallway was a dining room, its square dance floor surrounded by tables. A big oil stove gave forth a thrumming sound as the pipe fed in oil under pressure. Triggs quietly walked across to a telephone, dialed a number and said in a well-modulated voice, "Mr. Triggs speaking. Let me speak with Mr. Roper at once, please. . . . Hello. . . . Roper? This is Oscar. I have a couple of visitors out at my place, Douglas Selby, the district attorney, and Rex Brandon, the sheriff. They wanted in. I told 'em the place wasn't open yet, but they came in. . . . No, I don't think so." He turned away from the telephone, said calmly, "Hold the phone a minute," looked across at Brandon and asked, "You boys got a warrant?"

Brandon, his face flushed, moved aggressively forward.

Selby grabbed his coat, pulled him back. "When you've hung up that telephone," Selby said to Triggs, "we're going to talk."

"You could talk with my lawyer," Triggs said.

"We could," Selby told him, "but we're not going to."

Triggs turned back to the telephone. "No, apparently they haven't a warrant. They want to talk. . . . All right. . . . They claim it's a public place. How about that . . . ? Yes, it's open to the general public, only we ain't serving meals right now. . . . All right, Sam, thanks. I'll call you again if I need you. G'by."

Triggs hung up the telephone and said, "No hard feelings. I just wanted to know where I stand. My lawyer says you can come into the dining room. That's open to the public. You can't come into my office or my living quarters. They're not open to the public. You can't do any searching."

Brandon said truculently, "We'll go anywhere we damn please."

"Okay," Triggs remarked, taking a package of cigarettes from his pocket. "That's up to you. You can argue about it afterwards in court when I sue your bondsmen. Have a cigarette, gents."

Selby said, "Evidently you have something to conceal out here, Triggs."

Triggs said, without raising his voice, "Don't pull that old line of hooey with me. I wasn't born yesterday, and this isn't the first road house I ever ran. In the city I get by okay. Out here in the sticks you fellows want to show your authority. I know damn well you came out to throw a scare into me, and I'm here to tell you I don't scare worth a damn. I'm running a legitimate business. Incidentally, if you want to get wise to yourself, you'd realize that I'm a benefit to the community. I buy all my supplies in Madison City. I pay cash for my stuff. I take money from the chaps who are coming through in automobiles. If it weren't for my place, they'd go whizzing through *your* town in high gear. As it is, I . . ."

"Yes," Selby interrupted drily, "you're a public benefactor. We know all about that, Triggs. Now then, I'll do the talking and *you* can do the listening. It takes all sorts of people to make a world. You can't change human nature by legislation. I know that. But we have laws, and I'm elected to help enforce those laws. We can't enforce all of them. There's going to be *some* gambling in spite of anything we can do. There'll be commercialized vice. We couldn't stamp it all out if we had an army under us. But I *can* tell you this: When you start corrupting young boys, you've gone too damn far. You're running a gam-

bling game out here. I don't know how big it
is, but I know it's here. Now, there are some people in
Madison City who don't think there's anything wrong
with a friendly poker game. I'll have a hard time getting
evidence on you, and I'll have a hard time getting a conviction after I get the evidence, but there are ways of doing it. If I want to badly enough, I can put you on a spot.
Now then, I'm warning you once and for all: Lay off the
young folks in Madison City."

"More specifically," Triggs said calmly, "what are you
driving at?"

"Ross Blaine," Selby told him. "He gave a forged
check so he could buy chips in a game out here."

Triggs said slowly, "I'm sorry about Blaine. He has
no business coming out here. It won't hurt my feelings
any if you tell him to keep off the premises. This is a
business establishment, not a lounging place for kids who
haven't a nickel to spend."

"I believe he comes out here with George Stapleton
doesn't he?" Selby asked.

"Stapleton's different. Stapleton knows his way
around, and he has money to spend."

"Any personal reason you don't like Blaine?" Selby
asked.

Triggs avoided the question. "Of course," he said, "if
Blaine's a friend of yours and *you* want him around
here . . ."

"I don't want him around here," Selby said.

"All right, then, neither do I."

Selby said, "And I don't want any professional gamblers coming in here from Los Angeles."

"I wouldn't let one of them come on the place," Triggs
assured him. "I want to run a clean road house."

Selby said ominously, "I don't think you're trying very
hard to co-operate, Triggs. You can consider this visit as
a warning."

"All right," Triggs said. "It's a warning."

"You're skating on thin ice, Triggs," the sheriff said.

"And you're hoping I don't fall in," Triggs said sarcastically.

Selby took Rex Brandon's arm. "Come on, Rex," he said, "let's go. I think we've said everything we want to."

The sheriff hung back. Suddenly he whirled and said to Triggs, "I don't think you understand *us; but I know damn well we understand you!*"

Triggs walked across the room and held the outer door open for them. "Good morning, gentlemen," he said. "Come again. Drop in any time—that is, to the part that's open to the public."

He stood in the doorway, watching them until they had crossed the graveled parking space to the county car.

"Damn him!" Brandon said. "I should have hung one on his chin. Sam Roper's been filling him full of a lot of talk. He figures no twelve men in this county will convict him on a gambling charge. He's smart enough to buy all of his supplies in town and pay cash for them. A lot of the merchants figure just the way he says, that he isn't hurting the town any as long as he runs the road house outside of the city limits. They figure he's bringing money into the county and . . ."

"There are some ways of getting at him that Roper hasn't figured on," Selby interrupted. "He's going to want a renewal of his business license in a couple of months."

"That's so," Brandon said, his face breaking into a grin.

"And," Selby went on, "the next time this professional gambler comes in from Los Angeles, we're going to raid the place. We'll hold the players as well as Triggs. That'll give the people around here a chance to see what sort of a game Triggs is running."

They drove in silence for a few minutes. "Well, our hitch-hiker's gone," the sheriff pointed out. "Whatever his game was, he's figured this is a poor place to play it."

CHAPTER III

Let me off here," Selby told the sheriff. "I want to stop at the stationery store, and I'll walk up to the courthouse. The exercise will do me good."

Brandon obligingly slid the car into a parking space at the curb. "Let me know, Doug, when you're ready to go on that road house business."

Selby said, "It won't be long. You know me, Rex; I'm pretty much of a gambler myself. I like to see things move."

"I'll say you do," the sheriff told him. "Following you around during the campaign gave me a bunch of gray hairs. I never did know what you were going to do next."

"I didn't myself," Selby admitted with a reminiscent grin. "I always figured Sam Roper was a veteran politician with a pretty well-defined plan of action. I figured the only way to discount his political experience was to keep things stirred up enough so he'd never have a chance to get set. That made the campaign sort of extemporaneous—like reaching in a grab bag."

"I'll say it was a grab bag, and you grabbed the district attorneyship. . . . Well, let me know when we clamp the lid down on Triggs."

The county car slid into motion. Doug Selby entered the stationery store, bought some sheets for his notebook and emerged to the sidewalk just as a cream-colored car, resplendent with chrome steel, came purring along the street. The young woman at the wheel promptly slammed on the brakes, opened the door and asked, "How about a lift to the courthouse, Doug?"

Selby accepted the invitation with alacrity. "I've been thinking of you," he said to Inez Stapleton as he slid in beside her, "and wondering how I could get in touch with you."

She turned dark, observant eyes to his profile. Her trimly shod foot pushed down the clutch pedal as she snapped the lever into second gear. "We're listed in the telephone book," she remarked, "and, after all, they've taken the smallpox sign down, you know. You *could* come up to see me once in a while without being quarantined."

Selby laughed, watched the deft motions of her hands and feet as she guided the big car swiftly through the traffic. There was, he reflected, something puzzling about her. Her muscular actions were bewilderingly swift. He knew, to his sorrow, that on the tennis court her mind and arm co-ordinated with amazing speed. But in conversation, she rarely gave a quick answer. Usually, there was a flashing glance of appraisal from her dark eyes, then a split second as though she were debating which line of attack or defense to rely upon, and then her answer—usually disconcerting.

She was five years older than her brother, slender, well-formed, closely knit, and with a figure which seemed designed to show smart clothes to the best advantage.

"Well?" she asked, flashing him another one of those quick glances, "are you going to be charitable and donate your thoughts, or do I pay a penny for them?"

"I was thinking," Selby said, "of something I heard a woman say about you the other day."

"Aha!" she told him, "one sure-fire way to make a suppliant out of the proudest woman. Tell me, Doug, what did she say?"

"She said," Selby told her, "that no matter what Inez Stapleton had on, you never thought of her as being *dressed*. You always thought of her as being *gowned*."

Inez laughed lightly and tried vainly to keep the pleasure from her voice. "She should have seen me in the garden this morning," she said, "wearing overalls and inspecting frost damage. . . . Lord, it was cold last night, Doug!" He nodded, as she deftly swung the steering wheel, depressed the throttle, and sent the car slewing around the turn and charging up the Madrone Avenue hill. "So you *were* thinking about me?" she inquired.

"Yes. I wanted to talk with you about your brother."

She flashed him a glance, then looked back at the road. Her mouth became firm. "Yes?" she said, noncommittally.

"I wonder if George isn't cutting a pretty wide swath," Selby said.

She drove for half a block with her eyes straight on the road. Then she said banteringly, "Doug, I despair of you. Before you got into politics you used to come and see me. We used to play tennis, hike and ride together. Then you throw your hat into the political arena, become the fighting young district attorney, and immediately avoid me as though I had the plague. Then I see you, and my heart goes all pitty-pat because you say you have been looking for me—and it turns out you want to consult me about my brother. . . . I take it your interest is purely professional?"

He laughed apologetically and said, "You know, this job is—well, I don't dare to fall down on it, Inez."

"I see," she observed in a tone which indicated she didn't see at all.

She swept around the turn into Coleman Street and slid into a parking place in front of the courthouse. "Very well," she said, "since your interest in me is purely professional, Mr. District Attorney, the ride is over. Here you are at your destination."

"You still haven't answered my question," Selby said. "I don't know whether you're avoiding it or just putting me on the defensive on general principles."

She said, "As if anyone could put *you* on the defensive."

Selby said evenly, "I asked you if your brother wasn't cutting a rather wide swath."

She flickered her eyes to his, paused for that customary judicious half second, as though debating how to answer him, and then said, "Perhaps he is, Doug. I wouldn't know. Dad's coming home tomorrow. I'm going to suggest he give George a job in the sugar factory and put him to work."

"Does George know what you have in mind?"

"No. Don't ever tell him where the suggestion came from."

"A professional confidence," he assured her.

She stared straight through the windshield, her right

foot alternately depressing and releasing the accelerator, drumming a little tune on the motor. "I wonder," she said slowly, "if it wouldn't be a good plan to have Dad find a job for *me*."

"Why?" he inquired facetiously. "Are *you* cutting a pretty wide swath?"

She remained serious, her eyes slightly pensive. "I notice," she remarked thoughtfully, "that you seem to have time only for working girls." Selby's forehead showed that he didn't understand. "At least," she went on, "I gather that's the reason we never see you any more."

"This is something of a job, Inez," Selby explained. "I don't have much spare time."

"What do you do Saturday afternoons and Sundays?"

"To tell you the truth, most of the time I'm up at the office."

She switched the subject abruptly. "I saw Sylvia Martin a couple of days ago. She's evidently making good as a reporter on *The Clarion*."

"I'll say she's making good!" Selby exclaimed, with swift pride. "That girl's a wonder. She's a hard worker, and she certainly has a head on her shoulders!" It wasn't until Inez Stapleton's silence had become noticeable that Selby realized he had, perhaps, been a trifle too enthusiastic. "I'm wondering," he said, steering the conversation into more impersonal channels, "if George isn't doing a bit of gambling and perhaps losing a good deal of money."

"I wouldn't know," she said listlessly. "George doesn't discuss his personal affairs with me. If I were five years younger instead of five years older than he is, the situation would probably be different. A boy likes to protect a kid sister, but as he grows up, he comes to look on an older sister as a wet blanket, always dampening his life, liberty and the pursuit of adventure. Why don't *you* have a talk with George, if you feel worried about him, Doug?"

Selby said slowly, "He's spirited and high-strung, Inez. If I warned him directly, I think it might have the effect of making things just that much worse. In other words, he'd want to show me that he could take care of himself."

She ceased playing tunes with the motor.

"You *could* run out to the house to see me and casually drop a hint to George. After all, you know, your action wouldn't be entirely unprecedented. You *have* called on me before. Let's see, when was it?" She half closed her eyes and started counting on her fingers.

Selby laughed. "I surrender! Don't kick a man when he's down. When the weather warms up, let's take up our tennis again." He opened the car door and slid to the pavement.

"Am I to understand," she asked, "that I'm being invited for a tennis match some time in the early spring or late summer of the current calendar year?"

"Tomorrow's Saturday," he told her, "and Saturday afternoon's a half holiday."

She concealed the expression in her eyes by turning her head and looking out through the left-hand window, making a judicious appraisal of the smudge-smoked sky. "Well," she said, "it'll slow down my game some if I can't wear shorts, and this is goose-pimply weather. . . . Tell you what I'll do, Doug Selby. I'll just bet you that your eyes are so full of law books I can beat you two sets out of three. I'll bet you a trip to Los Angeles, a dinner, a show and an after-theater supper at a night club."

"That's taking an unfair advantage," he told her. "If I won, I wouldn't collect because I'd feel like a gigolo."

She turned toward him, then, her face a mask. "All right, Piker, get back to your old office and your stuffy law books. . . . And it's a date for tomorrow. At two o'clock?"

"At two o'clock," he assured her, "unless," he added jokingly, "there should be a murder between now and then."

She said tonelessly, "I knew there'd be a string to it somewhere," and assured herself of having the last word by snapping the car into reverse gear and leaving him no alternative but to close the door and watch her back the long length of the cream-colored automobile out from the curb and send it charging down the street as though it had been a spirited horse suddenly cut with an unexpected blow of the whip.

CHAPTER IV

THE SUN shone more warmly by noon. At eight o'clock the government meteorologist announced that a low pressure area, moving in from the coast, had definitely put an end to the cold spell. Farmers who had not had their clothes off for three days and nights tumbled into bed to sleep the sleep of utter exhaustion.

By midnight it had clouded up. At two o'clock in the morning the rattle of rain drops aroused the district attorney. He arose, adjusted the window so the rain wouldn't spatter in on the rug, and noticed that it had turned slightly warmer. The cold rain came pelting down in torrents, clarifying the smoke-laden atmosphere, and bringing relief to many a worried rancher.

At four o'clock, Selby was awakened by a steady, insistent ringing of his telephone. His eyes swollen with sleep, he took down the receiver and heard Sheriff Brandon's voice saying, "Doug, there's some trouble down at the Keystone Auto Camp. I think you'd better jump in your car and meet me down there."

"Good heavens," Selby said, "let the city police take care of it. It's probably a family fight of some sort and . . ."

"There's a dead man in one of the cabins," Brandon said. "He was evidently laying for someone with a gun—"

"I'll be there in fifteen minutes," Selby promised, and slammed the receiver up. He jumped into his clothes, grabbed a rain coat and cap from his closet, dashed down to the garage where he kept his car, and went roaring out into the rain. Madison City was virtually deserted. Along Main Street, a couple of all-night cafés catered to the through automobile trade. Night lights gave fitful illumination to store windows. Every alternate street light had been extinguished as an economy measure by the city trustees. But enough light remained to show the little mushrooms of water which arose from the pavement under the impetus of the driving rain drops.

Selby swung well over to the right, to avoid the inter-

24

urban street car tracks, and opened his car into
speed. His windshield wiper beat monotonously back and
forth. Rain streamed in torrents into the illumination of
his headlights. He ran through the boulevard stop at Pine
Avenue, and within three minutes had reached the city
limits. A hundred yards beyond, the arched sign of Key-
STONE AUTO CAMP showed mistily through the downpour. A car from the city police department was parked
near the last cabin. Sheriff Brandon's car was on the
other side of the building. Selby could hear the murmur
of voices and occasionally a shadow crossed the lighted
windows.

Selby parked his car behind the city police car and
Brandon opened a door and said, "Come in here, Doug."

Selby entered the cabin, which held two double beds,
a dresser and three chairs. Otto Larkin, the big, paunchy
chief of police, said, "Hello, Selby," and immediately
turned away to face two frightened young women who
sat side by side on a double bed. Both beds had been
slept in.

Rex Brandon studied the girls with thoughtful eyes
and said to Otto Larkin, "Now Selby's here, I think we'll
let him handle it."

Larkin said belligerently, "These two janes know the
answers. Don't let them kid you for a minute."

Brandon said softly but ominously, "After all, you
know, Larkin, the Keystone Auto Camp is outside the
city limits."

Larkin turned to stare indignantly at the sheriff. "All
right," he said, "if that's the way you want to play the
game, try and get any co-operation out of *me* in the future! When Roper was in office I always worked with
him. I was willing to work with you two. But if you . . ."

"Keep your shirt on, Larkin," Brandon said calmly.
"All I told you was that Selby was going to handle
things."

"What is there to handle?" Selby asked.

Brandon nodded toward the girls. Selby studied them.
One was a blonde. Her blue eyes showed that she had
been crying. As Selby looked at her, her lips quivered,

her fingers twisted at a handkerchief. The other girl was chestnut-haired, with brown eyes. She gave no evidence of having experienced any emotion whatever. She sat motionless, her eyes watching every move made by the officers.

Brandon indicated the blonde girl and said, "That's Audrey Prestone, Doug. The other one's Monette Lambert. Now, girls, this is the district attorney, and I want you to tell him exactly what you've told us."

Audrey Prestone looked beseechingly at Monette Lambert, who met Selby's eyes and said quietly, "The truth is, Mr. Selby, that we know absolutely nothing about it. We came up here with two boys, Tom Cuttings and Bob Gleason. We're going yachting with them tomorrow out of Los Angeles. We told the boys we wanted a separate cabin. They were nice about it. They gave us this cabin and they took the one adjoining.

"They knew some boys up here, George Stapleton and Ross Blaine. They did some telephoning. We didn't hear it. They told us we were to have a get-together at the Palm Thatch, which is a road house half a mile or so down the road. We went down there and stayed until a little after midnight. We were pretty tired and naturally didn't want to meet the women on the yachting party tomorrow looking as though we were something the cat had dragged in. We insisted on the boys' bringing us back here. We said good night and they went over to their cabin. We went to ours. We didn't take very long creaming our faces and getting into bed. We were dog-tired. I got up about half an hour ago, perhaps a little earlier, and saw light coming from a curtained window in the boys' cabin. I thought perhaps one of them was sick. It was raining. I put on my shoes and threw a coat over my pajamas, ran across to the other cabin, and knocked on the door. There was no answer. I looked through the window. There was just an inch or so between the shade and the window that give me a chance to look into the cabin. I saw the beds hadn't been slept in. I could see a man's feet sticking out from behind the dresser. I ran back and wakened Audrey. Then we dressed and ran up

to the office. There's a booth outside with a
dial telephone. We telephoned the police. That's all we
know."

"Where are the boys now?" Larkin asked.

"We don't know."

"You said good night to them?" Larkin asked, skeptically, "at a little after midnight?"

"That's right."

"*How* did you say good night?" the police chief
wanted to know, his voice showing his skepticism, "by
waving your handkerchief at them, or . . . ?"

Monette Lambert looked him straight in the eyes and
interrupted him to say, "How do you think a girl says
good night to a man when she's out on a trip with him?
We kissed them."

"Now we're getting somewhere," Larkin said. "You
did a little necking, didn't you?"

"I don't know what *you* call necking," Monette Lambert said in firm, precise tones, which made no attempt
to disguise her disgust, "but we didn't do what *I* call
necking. We kissed them good night, and then came over
here and went to bed."

"In two double beds, I suppose," Larkin said.

"In two double beds," she repeated evenly.

Selby said, "I think I'll handle it, Larkin, if you don't
mind." Larkin, with an exclamation, turned away. "Did
the boys say whether they intended to go out again?"

She surveyed Selby with appraising eyes. Her voice
was less quietly ominous. "They didn't say a thing," she
told him. "We supposed, of course, they were going to
bed. I don't think they *said* they were, and I'm quite certain they didn't say that they weren't. How about it,
Audrey, did you hear them say anything at all
that . . . ?"

The other girl shook her head in vigorous denial,
raised a handkerchief to her eyes and sobbed quietly.

Rex Brandon said, "We got into the place, Doug. I'd
been out on a call in the east end of town, so it happened
I had my clothes on when I telephoned you. I came right
down. That hitch-hiker we saw yesterday afternoon was

lying dead in the cabin. He'd evidently hidden behind the dresser and was waiting for someone to come in. He had a gun in his right hand and a printed note all ready to pin on the body. It's a goofy note and . . ."

"And what killed this man?" Selby interrupted to ask.

"The gas heater," Brandon said. "He'd closed the place up tight and started the gas heater going, to keep warm while he was waiting. The heater was going full force. It's a cheap tin affair and out of adjustment, at that. When we opened the door, it was like opening the door of a gas oven. We've aired the place out and have left things just the way they were, for the coroner. I've telephoned him and he should be here any minute."

Selby said, "Let's take a look. Can I trust you girls to stay here?"

"Why not?" Monette Lambert asked.

"You *might* go away," Selby told her.

"Where to?" she asked.

"Oh, just places."

"How?"

Selby laughed and said, "We won't even bother to argue about it. I'm putting you girls on your honor."

Otto Larkin said, "These girls know a lot more about this than they're telling. Personally, I don't think the boys ever went near that cabin. That second cabin was just a blind. I'll bet they ducked out when the girls were telephoning to headquarters."

"All right," Selby said quietly, "that's *your* theory. It's the policy of *my* office not to accuse any young woman of anything which will result in unfavorable publicity unless I have some proof. Come on, Larkin, you'd better come with us."

Larkin controlled himself with an effort. "That's all right, Selby. No hard feelings. I guess we all of us look at things different, that's all. Anyhow, I've had quite a bit of experience . . . maybe too damn much . . . maybe I get too skeptical. But I don't like the way these janes tell their story. I don't like the picture here. I tell you, those two guys got up not over an hour ago and went out to build up an alibi someplace. When you find them, they'll swear they've been playing cards or something ever since midnight. You'll probably find them back at the Palm Thatch with a manufactured alibi."

"Thanks for the suggestion," Selby said quietly.

"Okay," Larkin said, "it's outside of the city limits. I'm on my way. I wish you boys luck." He opened the door, turned up the collar of his raincoat and plunged out into the downpour.

"You girls will stay here?" Selby asked.

"Yes."

Selby said, "Come on, Rex. Let's go," and stepped out into water-soaked, soft gravel. They crunched their way across to the adjoining cabin, cold rain beating into their faces. Brandon took a key from his pocket and inserted it in the door. "This the key to the cabin?" Selby asked.

"No, it's a passkey."

"How about the man who runs the place? What . . . ?"

"Jimmy Grace," Brandon said. "He's out somewhere. Apparently the cabins were all rented and Jimmy went to Los Angeles or someplace. We can't raise anyone in the office. All right, Doug. Here we are. I haven't touched anything. I'm leaving it for the coroner. I moved the dresser a little bit so we could get to the man. When I saw he was dead, I didn't touch anything. Of course, I shut off the gas heater and opened the windows."

The cabin was identical with the one they had just left. There were two double beds, a dresser, a door leading to the bathroom, and another door leading to a kitchenette with an iron sink, a three-burner gas plate, and shelves stained in a natural finish.

A man, who had evidently been standing, concealed behind the dresser in the corner of the room, had slumped down into a grotesque sitting position. His right hand rested on a blued-steel .38 caliber revolver. His left hand held a long pin such as florists give with corsages. A sheet of paper was on the floor some two feet away.

"I decided we wouldn't pick up the paper," Brandon said. "We'll leave everything just the way it is for the coroner. You can stand over here and read it."

Selby saw that the paper was a plain white sheet, on which had been laboriously printed in pencil:

I HAVE KILLED THIS MAN BECAUSE HE DESERVED TO DIE—I AM LEAVING THE GUN WITH WHICH I KILLED HIM BESIDE THE BODY SO THE WORLD WILL KNOW THAT I HAVE COMPLETED THE MISSION WHICH WAS ENTRUSTED TO ME. IF I AM CAUGHT I WILL NOT RESIST ARREST, NOR WILL I LIE ABOUT WHAT I HAVE DONE. BUT THE LAW WILL NEVER REACH ME BECAUSE THE LAW WILL NEVER BE ABLE TO TELL WHY I KILLED HIM. IF THE LAW HAD KNOWN THAT, I WOULDN'T HAVE HAD TO KILL HIM. MY VICTIM HAS NEVER SEEN ME IN HIS LIFE, AND YET BEFORE HE DIES, HE WILL KNOW WHY HE IS BEING KILLED. I AM THE FORCE OF RETRIBUTION. VENGEANCE IS MINE, SAITH THE LORD—BUT I HAVE BEEN CHOSEN AS THE AGENT OF DIVINITY. I HAVE KILLED, BUT I HAVE DONE NO WRONG.

"You see," Brandon said, "there's a pinhole in the top of that paper. He evidently was holding it in his left hand, ready to pin it on the body."

"Then his intended victim must have been one of these boys, either Cuttings or Gleason," Selby said.

"Looks that way."

Selby moved slowly around the cabin. "There are no marks of violence on him, Rex?" he asked.

"I don't think so," Brandon said. "Notice the color of his lips. He died from carbon monoxide poisoning. You can see what a rusty contraption this gas heater is. It shouldn't ever be turned on over half force, but it was going full blast, with the tips of the flames spreading out around the top."

"How about this whiskey bottle and the three glasses?" Selby asked, indicating a quart bottle and glasses.

"Those were on the dresser when we came in. It looks as though the boys had a drink before they left." Selby smelled the glasses. "I'm going to have a finger-print man see what he can get from them," Brandon said. "I've already telephoned him and he should be here any time now. He and the coroner will probably come together."

Selby frowned and said, "There are three whiskey glasses, Rex. If the boys had had a drink before they started out, there'd only be two glasses."

"There are the girls," Brandon suggested.

"Then there'd have been four."

"Well," the sheriff said, "the only other way to figure it is that the boys came in and had a drink with the man who was intending to murder one of them."

Selby suddenly bent down to look at the man's shoes. "What time did it start raining, Rex?"

"Around two o'clock."

"The man's shoes are dry. He must have been in here for around an hour and a half, then, before he was discovered."

"I get you, Doug," the sheriff said. "That's a good point."

Selby said, "It's the hitch-hiker, all right. What was it he said his name was, something that commenced with a W . . . ?"

"Emil Watkins," Brandon said. "I wish now I'd taken him in and given him a good shake-down. . . . But he didn't have that gun with him yesterday afternoon. I'll swear to that."

"Have you looked through his pockets?" Selby asked.

"No. The coroner likes to be present when that's done. . . . Of course, Doug, there's nothing to this as far as we're concerned. It's a case of a man who lay in wait to kill someone. He died while he was waiting for the victim to show up. That lets us out. But it's a case which'll attract a lot of newspaper attention. This man was some sort of a crank. Naturally, the newspapers will do a lot of speculating about who he was planning to kill."

Selby nodded. "All right, Rex. If that's the case, the dead hitch-hiker isn't half as important as the person he intended to kill. In other words, the hitch-hiker's dead. The man he intended to kill is alive. Let's find out something about the motivation."

"I don't see as *that's* so frightfully important, now the man's dead," Brandon said.

Selby indicated the whiskey glasses. "For one thing,

Rex, it's important because that's the thing the newspapers will want to know about. It's a lot better to have us find out and tell the papers, than for the papers to find out and tell us. In the first place, I'm not so certain about this thing. Apparently there were three men in this room. You can't figure the murderer having a drink with his intended victims, or with his intended victim and one other person. Now then, just suppose there was a conspiracy to kill someone. Suppose three people were in on it. The hitch-hiker is only one. He was the one who was chosen to do the actual killing. The other two furnished the place for him to wait. Evidently, then, they intended to bring the victim here to him. If that's the case, it leaves two potential murderers at large who . . ."

"Okay," Brandon said, "I get your point. What do you want to do?"

"You have a deputy coming down here to look around for finger-prints. Harry Perkins, the coroner, is on his way down. Personally, I think those girls will stay put for a few minutes. I'm not so certain about Otto Larkin. I think he'd like to show us up by beating us to the punch. What do you say we get down to the Palm Thatch before he does?"

"Do you think the boys are down at the Palm Thatch?"

Selby nodded. "Stapleton and Blaine were down there. They evidently hadn't gone home. The boys went back to join the party."

"Of course," Brandon remarked dubiously, "there may be something to that point Otto Larkin made, that the boys went dashing out some place to build an alibi for themselves."

"If they did that," Selby said, "the place they'd go to do it would be the Palm Thatch."

Brandon stared at the sprawled figure of the lifeless hitch-hiker for a moment in thoughtful silence. The beating of rain on the roof of the cabin made a sinister undertone of sound. There was none of the gentle, hypnotic drowsiness of a warm rain, but a cold, ominous downpour which somehow seemed definitely hostile.

Selby shook himself against the damp chill which was creeping in through the half open windows. A siren, close at hand, moaned into a subdued signal. Brandon's face showed relief. "Here they come now," he said. "Okay, Doug, let's go to the Palm Thatch."

CHAPTER V

RAIN was falling in torrents as Selby, following the sheriff's car, pulled up in front of the Palm Thatch. The neon sign had been switched off, but flood-lights illuminated the parking ground and showed the bedraggled tips of the palm leaf thatch from which the water poured in streams. Rex Brandon and Doug Selby sloshed through the wet gravel to the porch. Brandon reached for the bell button. Selby said, "Just a minute, Rex. Let's try the door." He turned the knob. The door was unlocked. Selby pushed it open and the two men entered the reception hall.

There were no lights on in the main dining room, but light filtered through a curtained doorway in the rear. Selby could hear cards being shuffled, and the rattle of chips. He nodded to Rex Brandon. Quietly, on tiptoe, they crossed the dining room and paused at the green curtain which hung across the doorway. ". . . going to raise you an even hundred," a man's voice said. "I'm staying," another remarked, while a third said, "And *up* a hundred."

The voice of a young man said, "That first hundred used up the last of my chips. I'll give you my I O U for a hundred and see the raise."

"You're calling?" the man's voice asked.

"Yes, I'm calling."

Selby waited a few silent seconds, then nodded to Brandon. They jerked back the curtain and stepped into a private dining room. Seven men were grouped about a table which was illuminated by a single light hanging from a drop cord and enclosed in a conical shade of green glass with an inner opalescent reflecting surface.

Selby recognized the profile of George Stapleton, the back of Ross Blaine's head and neck, the bald head of Oscar Triggs. The other four were strangers to him. There were two young men in the early twenties, a heavy-set, florid, well-dressed, middle-aged man with large blue eyes, a close-cropped gray mustache, and a genial expression of beaming, frank good nature; another man in his forties, dark, thin-faced, long-fingered. His wavy, black hair swept back from a high forehead. His mouth was a thin, straight line. His eyes were restless, constantly on the move, watching everything and everyone. He was the one who first saw Selby and Rex Brandon.

"Couple of customers, Triggs?" he asked, in a quiet, well-modulated voice, a slight raising of his finely arched eyebrows indicating the two men.

Triggs whirled, pushing his chair back as he got to his feet. "This is the law," he announced quietly.

Selby moved forward and said, "Don't touch anything."

The dark man stretched forth a long arm. His fingers circled about the chips in the center of the table. Selby jerked the arm aside, and scattered the chips. "I want this," he said, picking up an oblong of paper.

Triggs walked around the table. "You can't pull this stuff. I told you to get a warrant if you wanted in. This place is closed and the doors are locked. You picked a lock and . . ."

"We picked nothing," Brandon said. "Get back there and sit down!"

Selby spread out the oblong of paper, read, "I O U one hundred dollars. George Stapleton." Selby folded the paper, pushed it down in his vest pocket. Triggs moved toward him and said, "You can't take that without a warrant."

Brandon, pushing between them, grabbed Triggs by the shoulders and said, "I told you to get back there and sit down!"

Triggs regarded the sheriff for a moment with cat-green eyes which showed nothing of his feelings, then he quietly turned, walked back to his chair, and sat down. "The tall young fellow's Doug Selby, the district attorney," he announced tonelessly. "The hard-boiled guy is the sheriff. They've entered without a warrant. The front door was locked and the place closed to business. You fellows remember that when the case comes up."

The dark, slender man said suavely, "We weren't playing for money anyway. It was just a sociable game for chips while we were waiting for the rain to let up."

Selby indicated the vest pocket in which he had placed Stapleton's I O U for one hundred dollars, and said, "Try telling that to a jury in this county and you'll be indicted for perjury."

The elderly man with the china-blue eyes said in a resonant voice, "What's the matter, Oscar? Don't you have any law in this county? I thought officers had to get a warrant before they could bust in on a friendly game of cards."

Selby said calmly, "Not that I give a damn, but I'm correcting you on one thing: That door was unlocked."

"I put the night-latch on myself," Triggs said.

"Well, then someone snapped it off," Selby told him, "because it was unlocked and we walked in. Now then, we're looking for a couple of boys who have a cabin at the Keystone Auto Camp."

One of the young men said, "Yes, we have a cabin at the Keystone."

"What's your name?"

"Tom Cuttings."

"Where do you live, Cuttings?"

"Down in Mirande Mesa."

"I think I've heard of you before," Selby said. "Didn't you play on the football team with Stapleton?"

"Yes, sir."

"And bought Stapleton's car, didn't you?"

"Yes, sir, the one in the shed outside, the red convertible with the white trim."

"Put it in the shed to keep it out of the rain?" Selby asked.

"No, sir. I didn't have any idea it was going to rain when we came in. It looked a little cloudy, that's all. I always try to keep it under cover."

"What's your name?" Selby asked the other young man.

"Robert Gleason."

"What were you two doing here?"

Cuttings said frankly, "Playing poker, sir."

Selby said, "That's a lot better. Now then, I'm going to ask you some questions. I want truthful answers. When did you two get to the Keystone Auto Camp?"

"About nine-thirty tonight, the first time," Cuttings said.

"What did you do there?"

"We picked out a couple of cabins, put the baggage inside, and then all of us came out here to get something to eat."

"Whom do you mean by 'all of us'?"

Cuttings exchanged glances with Gleason. "Come on," Selby said. "Out with it."

"There are two girls with us," Cuttings said.

"How long did you stay out here?"

"Until around midnight."

"Then what did you do?"

"The girls got tired and wanted to go back home. George Stapleton tipped us off that there was going to be a game running after a while and asked us if we wanted to get in on it. We told him we did. So we took the girls back to their cabin. We had the adjoining cabin. I guess they were afraid we might be on the make. We heard them lock the door, then I tipped the wink to Bob and we sneaked out."

"What time was that?"

"About twelve-thirty."

"And when did you next go back to the cabin?"

"We haven't gone back."

"Didn't you go back about an hour ago?"

"Why, no, sir."

"Haven't you been back there since it started to rain?"

"No, sir. We've been right here all the time."

Triggs watched the district attorney with calm, unblinking eyes. "The two boys have been right here. I can vouch for that."

Ross Blaine glanced significantly at the district attorney. "They've been in and out," he said. "The game here's only been running about an hour. We've been sitting around, talking and having an occasional drink. The radio was on in the other room. A couple of girls were out here until about an hour ago. We did some dancing and some wandering around. I don't think anyone can vouch for where anyone has been, if you want to put it that way."

Triggs said in a conversational voice, "Getting to be quite a stool pigeon, aren't you, Ross?"

Ross Blaine made no effort to conceal the burning hatred in his eyes. "Keep on asking for things," he said to Triggs, "and you'll get them."

"Not from you," Triggs told him, "and from now on this place is closed to you. You don't need to come out here at all."

"I'll come in here any time I damn please," Blaine told him. "As long as it's open to the public I can come in and spend my money."

"*Your* money!" Triggs sneered. "A couple of beers, and you want to stay all night."

Stapleton entered the conversation. "Look here, Triggs, I resent that. God knows *I've* spent enough money in your joint, and Blaine comes out here as a friend of mine."

"You *think* he's a friend of yours," Triggs said calmly.

Blaine got to his feet with such violence that he sent his chair crashing backward. Sheriff Brandon reached forward and caught him by the coat collar. "Officially, Ross," he said, "I'm stopping you. Personally, I hate to do it."

Blaine squirmed for a moment, then subsided. Triggs looked up, apparently about to say something, but as his eyes met the sheriff's, he left the words unsaid.

The dark man said, "As far as I'm concerned, I'm an outsider. You've caught me sitting at a table where there were some playing cards. You *may* be able to make out a case against Stapleton because of the I O U, but you can't prove *I* was in the pot. You can't prove *I* was playing for money. And you won't get any admissions out of me. If the rest of you fellows want to take a little advice from me, you'll quit answering questions right now."

Selby turned to him and said, "I think I want to talk with you about another matter. In the meantime, you look like a man who likes to bet, so I'll bet you ten to one you're a professional gambler. I'll bet you even money you have a police record, and I'll bet you a million to one that if you start speaking out of turn you'll wish you hadn't." Without waiting for him to answer, Selby turned to Ross Blaine and said, "How long's the game been running, Ross?"

"A little over an hour. Mr. Needham"—indicating the genial individual with a nod of his head—"is a retired broker from Los Angeles. He got here about an hour and a half ago. He was looking for excitement and a poker game. I told him I wasn't playing. About twenty minutes later, Carlo Handley"—indicating the dark-visaged man —"just *happened* to drive in, by one of those rare coincidences which happens regularly every time Needham shows up here."

Triggs said significantly, "*Now* I know who left the door unlocked."

"That's a damn lie!" Blaine retorted.

The sheriff, still holding Blaine's collar, said, "Go over to that chair, Ross, and sit down."

Selby turned to Cuttings. "You boys are making pretty much of an all night party of it, aren't you?"

Cuttings glanced over at Gleason, then blurted, "Shucks, there wasn't anything else to do."

Gleason laughed, a short, nervous laugh.

Stapleton said, "I think I can explain, Mr. Selby. The boys planned a weekend. They were to make up a party and do some cruising on a friend's yacht. He told them to bring their girls along. The boys thought it'd be a lark to bring a couple of local girls, and asked these two.

They jumped at the chance. The boys planned to stop over here and have a little get-together with dancing and a few drinks. You know, just a jolly good time. Well, first rattle out of the box, one of the girls got sore at a story I told, and then they started in being regular wet blankets. They wanted to get their sleep so they'd look well on the yacht tomorrow, and nothing would do but the boys had to take them home. So I got the boys off to one side and suggested that if they'd sneak back here, I thought there'd be a little action later on."

Selby shifted his eyes back to Gleason. "Did you two boys have anyone else with you?"

Gleason said, "Just the two girls."

"No other man?"

"No."

"Something was mentioned about a couple of girls being out here."

Stapleton said, "They were a couple from Los Angeles. They come up here sometimes and you can pick them up."

Triggs said evenly, "You can't pick them up unless you look good to them. All they want is a chance to dance. They live out of town. I think they're married and like to come up to be on their own. Naturally, they like to have the boys look them over and sometimes they dance. When it comes bedtime they go home. You can't make anything out of those two girls."

"You boys didn't leave anyone in your cabin?" Selby asked Gleason.

"No, of course not. What are you driving at?"

"You came back out here to see Stapleton?" Selby asked Cuttings.

"Well, that's the reason we stopped over here on our way to Los Angeles. Then I came back out here because it seemed to me altogether too early to go to bed and . . ."

"And did you intend to take Stapleton back to the cabin with you?" Selby asked.

"Take Stapleton back to the cabin!" Cuttings repeated, his voice indicating puzzled bewilderment.

Ross Blaine said quietly, "*I'm* the one they invited to go back to the cabin with them—in case it makes any difference, Mr. Selby."

Cuttings blurted, "Why, we didn't . . . Oh, yes, we did too! I said if you didn't want your mother to hear you coming in this late at night you could come down and stay with us. I didn't mean it as an invitation, particularly."

"And," Handley said, his voice indicating that he had suddenly taken a deep interest in the affair, "you two boys suggested that you might as well make a night of it and get some sleep on the yacht tomorrow. You said in case Needham and I wanted to, *we* could go down and take your cabin."

"Well, yes, we did that, too," Cuttings said. "We're going to have to start for Los Angeles by seven o'clock, and we figured we'd get some sleep on the yacht. There won't be anything doing there until tonight, anyhow."

"Your friend must keep his yacht in commission all winter," Selby said.

"He does. It's a big hundred-and-twenty-footer and she smashes right through anything. Lots of times right during the middle of winter you get some good cruising weather. When it isn't good cruising weather, we hang around in the harbor, sing songs, play cards and do a little drinking. There's a bunch of real good scouts aboard. If the weather's at all favorable, we run over to Catalina, or sometimes take longer cruises down to Ensenada."

Selby said, "Look here, I want to know *exactly* what time you two boys got back here at the Palm Thatch."

A woman's voice from the curtained doorway said, "I think *I* can answer that question."

Selby whirled at the sound of her voice. She came smiling toward him, blonde, trim, graceful, poised, and apparently very sure of herself. Selby decided she had been standing just on the other side of the curtain, listening to the conversation. She was wearing a backless dinner gown of black, lacy material which emphasized her blonde hair and deep blue eyes. Her lips had been skillfully made up, the eyebrows were delicately arched.

"Permit me to introduce myself," she said, coming toward him. "I'm Madge Trent, the hostess here. And you, I suppose, are Mr. Selby, the district attorney." She smiled up into Selby's face, thrust warm, lithe fingers into his hand, and Selby noticed the freshly tinted, smoothly polished nails. She turned with a swiftly supple motion to Brandon, gave him the benefit of a quick smile which seemed entirely spontaneous, and said, "And you're Sheriff Brandon. I'm pleased to meet both of you. Now I think I can answer your questions about what happened here."

"Go ahead," Selby said.

"I'm on duty," she said, "as hostess. After the dining room is closed I have nothing to do. But I was in my room reading when I heard you come. I dressed, came down, and crossed the dining room in time to hear your question."

"We didn't hear you crossing the floor," Sheriff Brandon said.

"She's light on her feet," Triggs interposed hastily. "She's a professional dancer."

Madge Trent didn't take her eyes from Doug Selby. "The foursome which you seem interested in arrived here about ten o'clock," she said, "and I don't think the boys made proper allowances for the girls. The girls were working girls. I gathered from what they said they're secretaries. They'd had a hard day. Then they'd had a drive on top of that. They were particularly anxious to look their best when they got on the yacht tomorrow." She turned to Cuttings and said, "Now, how about it? You boys don't work, do you?"

Cuttings shook his head, grinning. "Our dads have orchards. The trees do the work."

"I thought so," she smiled. "And I'll bet you slept until around noon, didn't you?"

Gleason said, "Make it two o'clock this afternoon and you'd be nearer the mark. We knew we were going to have a big night, so we rested up for it."

"Exactly!" Madge Trent said. "I could see the girls were tired. They were just dog-tired. The whole thing was a bit strange to them and I think they began to worry about just what was expected of them. Anyway, they wanted to go home right at midnight. The party left here at five minutes past twelve. The boys were back here at half past twelve. I know, because I'm the one who let them in. When they rang the bell, I thought it was another party coming in and I looked at my watch to see what time it was."

Cuttings said, "Nothing's happened to the girls, has it? They haven't . . . that is, they didn't get to worrying about us, did they?"

Selby said, "Which one of you boys knows a man by the name of Emil Watkins?"

The young men exchanged blank, surprised stares. Gleason shook his head. Cuttings said, "I certainly don't."

"Do you know anyone by the name of Watkins?"

"No, sir," Gleason said.

"I know a Watkins in San Francisco," Cuttings said, "but I haven't seen him for years."

"The man I'm talking about is around fifty years old, with gray eyes, light hair, high cheekbones, and thin lips. He's about five feet seven, and only weighs about a hundred and thirty-five pounds. He may be the father of some girl you boys know. Do you know any girls named Watkins?"

In the impressive silence which followed, the boys answered in the negative by slowly shaking their heads.

Selby said, "I want you boys to take a look at this man and see if you know him."

"Why, I'll be glad to," Cuttings said. "Where is he?"

Selby said impressively, "I think by the time you boys get your things on the body'll be at the coroner's office."

"At the coroner's . . ." Cuttings' voice trailed off into silence. The members of the little party grouped about the table became suddenly motionless.

Selby said to Rex Brandon, "You might take the boys back to the cabin first, Rex, let them look the place over, and then meet me at the coroner's office. I'll go directly there. . . . And about those two girls, Rex: the party seems to have been pretty much on the up-and-up. Ap-

parently the girls are a couple of secretaries. It
wouldn't do them any good to have their names in the
papers. The business we're inquiring into, whatever it
was, seems to have centered around this cabin the boys
rented, so it might be a good plan to give those girls ·a
head start and let them get out of town before the newspaper reporters start asking questions and taking pictures."

Brandon nodded. "Okay, Doug," he said. Then, to the
boys, he said, "Come on, you two. Get your things on."

CHAPTER VI

SELBY slid his car in to the curb, turned up the collar of
his coat, and jabbed the bell on the door of the coroner's
office. He restrained an impulse to supplement the bell
ringing by pounding on the panels.

Harry Perkins, the coroner, was a tall, thin, bony-
faced individual who moved with a certain lanky grace.
He radiated homely efficiency, and regarded corpses with
detached impartiality. His hobby was trout fishing. He
opened the door, and said, "Hello, Doug. Ain't this a
peach of a rain? I like to see it come down this way. It
makes too fast a run-off for the farmers, but it's swell for
the streams. Get 'em all cleaned out early in the season
this way and it gives the fish a chance to run. . . . Here,
hang your coat over the chair. Let it drip."

"You have the body here?" Selby asked.

"You mean the chap from the Keystone Auto Camp?"

"Yes. I want to look him over."

"Right back this way."

"What've you found out about him?" Selby asked, as
they tramped along a dank, cold passageway, filled with
the odor of embalming fluid.

"Carbon monoxide gas, all right," the coroner remarked cheerfully. "It's funny how people *will* seal
themselves up in a room with a defective gas heater going full blast. If they only realized it, they can't get
warm that way, because so much oxygen is drained from

the air that it lowers their vitality. If they'd only be sensible and use gas the way it was intended to be used they'd have satisfactory heat. But they insist on turning it on full blast and trying to change the temperature in a whole room in a matter of seconds. Now, with a wood stove, it'd take a while to get the fire going, a while to get the stove hot, and the room would warm by degrees. With electricity, they'd expect to wait a while getting the room at proper heat. But with gas they want to light the match and have the temperature jump twenty degrees in twenty seconds. I never saw the beat of it."

"Find anything on him to show his identity?" Selby asked.

"Some letters addressed to 'Dear Dad,'" the coroner said. "Looks like he's been carrying 'em around with him for quite some spell."

"What's in the letters?"

"They're sort of pathetic," Perkins said. "Letters from a daughter who ran away and had a baby."

Perkins opened a door and said, "It's pretty cold in here, Doug. If you're going to stick around you'll have to get your coat. Personally, I don't think there's anything to stick around for. It's a plain case of carbon monoxide poisoning. There's his clothes hanging up. Here's everything that was in the pockets in this lock-box. The body's over here. Want to take a look at it?"

Selby nodded.

The coroner stripped back the covering. "Always easy to tell monoxide poisoning," he said. "The blood's a cherry red."

"No sign of violence on the body?" Selby asked.

"No, only a slight discoloration under the ear which might or might not be significant. For instance, it could easily be the result of a fall. B-r-r-r, it's cold in here. How about taking his stuff back to the office and going over it there?"

"Good idea," Selby agreed. "Let's go."

They switched out the lights and walked back down

the long corridor to the front office, the coroner carrying the lock-box. "I keep all the stuff in lock-boxes now," he said, grinning, "after the trouble we had with that other case. I'm not gonna take a chance on having anything substituted or stolen." Selby nodded.

The coroner opened the door of his office, gestured toward a gas heater and said, "That's the way a gas heater *should* be," and slid the lock-box over to the table. He opened it and said, "A jackknife, and, in case you're interested, it's good and sharp. They have a saying, you know, that a sharp knife means a lazy man. Thirty-five dollars in currency, a dollar and eighteen cents in coins, an old turnip watch running right on the second, the stub of a carpenter's pencil, a wallet, and these letters."

Selby took the three letters in his hand, removed them from a dirt-glazed envelope, unfolded them, and spread them on the coroner's desk. "No address on the envelope," he remarked, "or on the letters."

"No," Perkins told him. "The way I figure it, he carried them in his pocket for a while until they got pretty worn, and then he started putting them in envelopes. You can see this envelope is pretty nearly worn through on the edges, but the inside of it is all gray where the letters have been rubbing against it. So I figure the letters were pretty badly soiled before they were ever put in the envelope."

Selby nodded, stared at the letters, delayed unfolding them. "Do you know, Harry," he said, "this job has a strange fascination for me. I like to look into the lives of people. I used to think you could only tell about people when they were alive. Now I'm commencing to think you can only *really* learn about people after they're dead. All of their hypocrisies are dissolved in death."

"You'll learn a good deal about the man's daughter when you read those letters," Perkins said. "But I don't know how you figure you're going to find out much about men after they're dead."

"It's the little things," Selby told him, "the little indices of character. You mentioned a significant fact a moment ago when you said the knife was sharp, and called attention to the fact that a popular belief is a man whose knife is sharp is lazy."

"Oh, sure," Perkins agreed, "you can find out those things about a man after he's dead, but by that time no one cares."

Selby frowned at him thoughtfully. "Do you know, Harry, I'm commencing to believe that we should completely revolutionize our theories of crime detection. We don't pay enough attention to the clews which indicate character. We overlook the most significant thing of all, which is motivation. It takes a powerful motive to make one man kill another."

"I guess you're right," Perkins admitted, his manner showing that revolutionizing methods of crime detection caused him but little concern, "only this isn't a murder case. This is a case where murder was nipped in the bud."

Selby started to say something, changed his mind, picked up the first letter and read:

December 15, 1930

DEAR DAD: This is to let you know that I'm not going to be with you for Christmas or New Year's. In fact, Dad, I'm checking out.

I don't know whether it would have made any great difference if Mother had lived. I suppose, after all, it wouldn't. Things just happen and that's all there is to it. I know you've tried to be a good father to me. You probably won't believe it, but I've tried to be a good daughter to you. Don't think I don't love you, because I do, but I do think you're hopelessly old-fashioned. You think I'm completely lacking in the qualities a young woman should have. I think you're mid-Victorian, but I love you just the same. You think I'm going to hell in a hand basket, and I don't know whether you love me or not. There are some things you don't understand and probably never can understand about me. If Mother had lived, I think she'd have understood, because I think in many ways I'm Mother's girl.

Because I know you won't approve of what I'm planning to do, I won't tell you what it is, only that I'm checking out.

Please believe me that I love you just as much as I ever did, which is plenty. But I hate arguments. I know that you don't approve of me and that you won't approve of what I'm going to do. I don't want to argue with you about it. I don't want to have things come to a show-down which would mean that you'd pit your will and your ideas of what's proper against my will and my determination to live my own life. And so, Dad, I'm just writing to say good-by.

Lots of love.   MARCIA

Selby slipped that letter back into the envelope, picked up the second letter which was dated October 5, 1931, and which read:

DEAR DAD: Since writing you last December, I've done a lot of thinking. I'm beginning to understand something of what it means to be a parent. I don't suppose I can tell you so you'll understand, but, briefly, you're going to be a grandfather some time around Thanksgiving. I don't know whether the news will give you a thrill or whether it will make you furious. I have an idea it will do a little of both.

The boy I've been living with couldn't marry me because of his family. It's too long to explain in a letter and anyway it doesn't make any difference now. Of course, we were going to get married as soon as he could get the family mess cleared up. He left me a month ago. I still love him, but I don't want him back. I see him now for what he really is—a spoiled, selfish, inconsiderate wastrel.

Now, my child is going to have plenty of handicaps. For one thing, it will have to get along without a father. Therefore, I don't want to be the one who deprives it of its grandfather, but I'm very certain of one thing: My child is never going to be subjected to the same narrow-minded intolerance which warped my own outlook on life for so many years.

I don't blame you for it, Dad. I blame the environment of civilization. However, you have your viewpoint.

I can never understand it, and I know very well you'll never understand mine.

To my mind, there is no marriage other than love. When two people really and truly love each other, I think that's all the marriage they need. Having a justice of the peace stand up and mumble a few words doesn't change the underlying relationship. I love this man. I'm not going to tell you his name because it wouldn't do any good. I thought he was going to marry me. I thought that by this time I could write you that I was duly and legally married. And then perhaps you'd want to see me. As it is, I consider it's the same as though I'd been married and divorced.

Now then, what happens is up to you. If you want to see me, if you want to consider that the little newcomer is entitled to your love just as much as though some justice of the peace had collected a five-dollar fee for reading a few lines out of a book, put an ad in the personal column of the Los Angeles papers—I'm not in Los Angeles, but I'll arrange to know about it if you put in the ad.

But please understand one thing, Dad. You aren't to put in the ad unless you're prepared to go all the way. My child is the natural result of a relationship entered into in good faith and founded on love. If you can't see things that way, don't try to get in touch with me.

The third letter was dated July, 1937, and read:

Dear Dad: A lot of water has passed under the bridge since I wrote you last, and your failure to put an ad in the personal columns of the Los Angeles papers showed me how you felt.

My child was a little girl. I didn't want to release her for adoption, and yet for a while it seemed the only thing to do. Then the baby's father agreed to support her. Because of that, I've been able to keep my daughter—in a way—but it's a nightmare of a life. I only receive enough for her. I have to work to support myself. I see Baby at infrequent intervals for a few hours at a time. I'm her mother but I'm a visitor. Her home is really the school where she lives. The teachers in that school share in her life. They know all of the little, intimate things about her. I get only a part of those things, and get them second-hand. When I come to the school, "Mother is coming to visit."

In short, Dad, I've really been deprived of my daughter, and it's recently occurred to me that I've deprived you of yours. I realize now that the loss of your daughter in many ways must have hurt you as much as what's happened with my daughter has hurt me. But I also know you'll never admit it. You'll never even try to understand. Some day pretty soon, Dad, I'm going to come and talk with you. On one thing I'm absolutely determined. You'll never see your grandchild unless your attitude toward her is right. But as far as I'm concerned, your attitude doesn't make so much difference, and I do want to see you, Dad. I wonder if you want to see me. At any rate, don't be surprised if I come walking in on you one of these days. I'm a long ways from you. It's going to take a little while to get money together for traveling expenses.

Love and kisses from your wayward daughter, MARCIA

Selby almost reverently folded the letters, put them back in the worn, dirt-glazed envelope. "What a complex thing life is, Harry," he said to the coroner, "and how people grope through it, trying to do what's right, seeking for happiness, and so frequently being denied it because of misunderstandings.

"Look at this man, for instance. He loved his daughter. He cherished those letters. Think of the loneliness which must have gnawed at his heart. He carried those letters with him, read them until the mere handling of them had frayed the paper and made the writing dim. Yet, he couldn't bring himself to forgive her. Just a little more charity, just a little more human understanding and they could have been happy. With the grandfather working and helping support the child, she could have had her daughter with her. . . . Somehow, Harry, we must find that daughter, and I hope this man left enough of an estate so it will help her support the child."

"It doesn't look as though he had very much money," the coroner said. "His clothes are pretty shabby. There's the money in the wallet. That's not enough to bury him."

Selby said, "We stopped him on the road yesterday. He was hitch-hiking. Rex Brandon was going to put a vagrancy charge against him, and . . ."

"Did you find out who he was?" the coroner asked.

"He said his name was Emil Watkins."

"Well, there's nothing on him to prove it," the coroner said. "That's everything he had in his pockets, what you see there in the lock-box."

Selby picked up the articles, one at a time, studied them, and replaced them in the lock-box. "Here's a funny thing, Harry," he said, "the man didn't have any keys."

"That's so," the coroner said. "Come to think of it, he had a jackknife, a pencil, a wallet . . . and no keys."

"When you stop to think of it," Selby said slowly, "it's a significant fact, rather a pathetic index of the man's character—a man without a home, a man who had no place to go, a man who had no keys."

"Well," Perkins said, "lots of people haven't homes these days. . . . Say, Doug, did I tell you about catching that big trout from the pool just below the forks? You remember I told you I knew that big one was in there. He rose to a gray hackle, and then when I missed connections, went down to the bottom of the pool and sulked. I was in there with a couple of other chaps. You remember I was telling you?"

Selby nodded.

"Well," Perkins said, "I went back and caught him. He was a beauty. Weighed two and a half pounds, and just as a matter of sentiment, Doug, I caught him on the same fly I'd missed him with before. You know, trout are funny that way. They . . ." He broke off as the doorbell rang, followed by a pounding of fists on the door. "They'll always do that," Perkins said. "Just because it's dark they think the bell ain't enough. They'll ring the bell and then bang with their fists. During the daytime they just ring the bell."

He crossed the office, to open the door. Sheriff Brandon ushered the two white-faced young men into the office.

"Learn anything?" Selby asked of the sheriff.

Brandon shook his head. Selby said, "I want you boys to take a look at the dead man."

Neither of the boys said anything. Gleason shivered. His teeth chattered audibly. "Stand over by the stove," Selby said, "and get warm."

Gleason said, "I'd rather get it over with now."

"All right," Selby told him, "let's go."

They walked in solemn, silent procession down the long cold corridor to the room where the coroner turned back the sheet, to expose the man's face, Cuttings stepped up first to view the body, then shook his head and stepped to one side. Gleason, his lips tightly compressed, looked down at the dead man, then turned hastily away.

"Do you know him?" Selby asked.

Both heads shook in unison.

"Take a good look," Selby said. "Try and visualize what he'd look like alive, with his eyes open and standing on his feet. Go on, boys, he isn't going to hurt you." Again the boys looked, then turned away. "How long since you boys have seen Marcia Watkins?" Selby inquired conversationally.

Neither face gave any sign of expression. Cuttings said, "I don't know any Marcia Watkins."

"Neither do I," Gleason said.

"How did it happen this man was in your cabin?" Selby asked.

Cuttings said, "Look here, Mr. Selby, I'm on the square in this thing. I can't figure it out. I don't know what he was doing in our cabin. I don't know how he got in. The thing is a complete shock to me."

Selby said, "All right, boys, I'm not going to hold you, but I want you to promise that if I telephone and ask you to come back here, you'll come at once. Will you do that?"

Cuttings said, "We certainly will, Mr. Selby. You've

been pretty white in this thing and Bob and I will do anything we can to help out."

Brandon said, "Let me talk with you for a minute, Doug. We can leave the boys here."

"Can't we wait in the other room?" Gleason asked.

"No," Brandon said. "You boys stay here for a minute."

He led Selby out into the corridor. "I don't like the idea of turning those boys loose, Doug," he said. "The more you consider those three whiskey glasses, the more you have to figure they're mixed up in the thing some way."

"I know," Selby told him, "but the more we question them now, the more we show them how little we know. I think the thing to do is turn them loose. If they're trying to get away with anything, let's let them think they're getting away with it. In the meantime we'll be investigating. When we know all about the dead man, we'll call them back. Reading the letters that were in his pocket, I'm pretty certain that he's a conventional and obstinate father who had a very deep love for a daughter who ran away and had a baby. When we find out where he lived, we can get a line on his daughter. When we locate her, we'll find out who the father of the child was. Then we'll know who it was this man was trying to kill."

"It might have been Cuttings or Gleason for all we know," Sheriff Brandon said.

"It might have been, but they're too young to have run away with the daughter. Their faces certainly didn't show any flicker of expression when I mentioned the name of Marcia."

"These letters you mention were in his pocket?" Brandon asked.

"Yes."

"Okay," Brandon said, "you're the boss, Doug. I suppose you're going to follow your favorite hobby of reconstructing the life of the dead man." Selby nodded. "But," Brandon said, "suppose it turns out that he did want to murder either Gleason or Cuttings. There's nothing we can do about it. They haven't committed any offense."

Selby said, "Suppose Gleason and Cuttings know something, but don't know they know it. Suppose they were associating with the man this hitch-hiker wanted to kill . . ."

"I get you," Brandon said.

"Of course," Selby pointed out, "the key to the whole thing may have been lost if we can't reconstruct things so we can find out what they knew."

"Well," Brandon observed, "if that's the case, I guess there's nothing for us to do but to write the whole thing off the books."

. They returned to the room where the coroner was trying to entertain the two boys, telling them about a fishing trip he had taken in the summer. The boys were watching him with wide eyes and faces which indicated they weren't paying the slightest attention to what he was saying. "Okay," Brandon said, "you boys can go now."

They gained the door in swift strides, pell-melled down the corridor ahead of the officers. Cuttings turned at the outer door and said, "Any time you want us, Mr. Selby, you can get us. The sheriff knows where to reach us." He opened the door and they shot out into the driving rain.

Selby said to the sheriff, "Come on in and read these letters, Rex."

The three men entered the office. Selby handed the letters to Brandon, who started to skim through them, then, frowning, began to read more carefully. The telephone bell shattered the silence. The coroner scooped up the receiver, said mechanically and all in one breath, "Coroner - and - public - administrator's - office - Perkins-Funeral-Parlors-Perkins-talking." He listened a moment, then said to Selby, "This is for you, Doug."

Doug picked up the receiver and said, "Hello."

A woman's voice, sounding strangely muffled, said, "The district attorney?"

"Yes."

The woman spoke rapidly, still with that peculiar muffled effect, as though she were holding something in her mouth for the purpose of disguising her voice, "Don't let them pull the wool over your eyes about what happened in the Keystone Auto Camp," she said. "Keep on investigating until you find out all about the murder."

Selby said, "Just a minute. This isn't the district attorney himself. This is a deputy. I'll call the district attorney."

"Oh, yes, it's the district attorney, Mr. Selby. Don't think you can stall me into holding the phone while you trace the call."

"I don't know just what you mean by a murder. The man died before he had committed any murder. Therefore, there wasn't any . . ."

"That's what *you* think," she said. "If you really knew the truth, you'd find the murder had already been committed, and you're just playing into their hands by thinking . . ." For a split second, the woman halted her rapid-fire, almost hysterical barrage of words. It was as though something near her had alarmed her and she had paused to listen.

"All right," Selby said, "what . . . ?" He heard the slam of a receiver at the other end of the line. Selby started jiggling the hook. Perkins said philosophically, "Take it easy, Doug. This time in the morning you take the kind of service they give you."

Brandon looked up from the letters, his eyes narrowed. Selby rattled the receiver. A sharp, irritable voice said, "All right, all right. What is it? What number do you want?"

Selby said, "This is Selby, the district attorney. I'm at the Perkins Undertaking Parlor. A call came in for me just now. I want it traced."

"Just a minute," the girl said. "I'll see what I can do. Hold the phone." A few moments later she said, "I *think* that call came from the All Night Drug Company in the hotel building."

"Get them on the line," Selby said.

"Just a minute."

Selby could hear the sound made by a bell ringing at the other end of the line. After what seemed an interminable interval, a man's voice said, "All Night Drug."

Selby said, "Where's this phone located, in the prescription department, out in front, or . . ."

"In a booth," the man said. "Who is this?"

"Get this straight," Selby said. "This is Douglas Selby, the district attorney. A call came in from this telephone a minute or two ago. I want to know who placed that call."

"A woman," the man's voice said. "A man drove her up in an automobile. She came running in and I thought she wanted something. I started out from the prescription department, but she shook her head at me and sprinted over toward the phone booth."

"Did you see what she looked like?"

"She was young. She had on a rain coat, with a cape thrown over her head."

"What color was the rain coat?"

"Some dark color. Black, I think."

"Could you see whether she was blonde or brunette?"

"No, I didn't pay any attention to her face."

"About how old was she?"

"Lord! You've got me there," the man admitted. "She ran as though she was young, but I tell you I didn't look at her face. As a matter of fact, about all there was to see was two eyes, a nose and . . ."

"And she's gone now?"

"Yes, she sure has. The man who was waiting outside in the car honked the horn and she slammed the receiver up and sprinted across the floor in nothing flat."

Selby said, "Run outside, look up and down the street and see if you can see any sign of that car."

"Okay," the man said in an unhurried voice. "Hold the phone."

Selby could hear the leisurely pound of steps echoed in the telephone. Then, after a few moments, he could hear the steps coming back.

"No," the man said, in a voice which indicated he was

bored by the entire proceedings. "No cars in sight."

"You said a man was waiting outside in a car?" Selby asked.

"Yes."

"Did you see him?"

"Not plain. I just saw somebody out there."

"How do you know it was a man?"

"I don't know. A young woman wouldn't be out this time of night—well, it was someone, either a man or woman."

"Thank you," Selby said wearily, and dropped the receiver into place. He turned to Rex Brandon and said, "Some woman warning me that there was more to this Keystone Auto Camp business than appeared on the surface."

"Did she say something about a murder?" Brandon asked.

"Yes. From all I can gather, she has an idea the man had already committed a murder."

"You mean he'd murdered someone before the gas stove got him?"

"That's what I gathered she meant. Apparently she was interrupted in the middle of whatever she wanted to say."

"If he'd murdered someone," Brandon said, "why didn't he pin the note on the body? He had it all ready."

Selby shrugged his shoulders and said, "All I know is what she told me over the telephone. She appeared to be holding something in her mouth, as though trying to disguise her voice."

Perkins looked at Rex Brandon. "Suppose it was one of the girls those two boys had with them?"

Brandon turned thoughtful eyes to the district attorney. "Perhaps we're making a mistake letting those girls go, Doug," he said quietly. "One of them was a pretty cool customer."

"No," Selby said, "things are working out all right. Turn them loose and give them plenty of rope. If we'd detained them for questioning they wouldn't have given out any information at all. As it is, this anonymous tip shows *someone* is interested in having the true facts brought to light."

"If he's murdered the man he was after, where do you suppose he put the body?" the sheriff inquired.

Selby looked at his wrist watch. "Well," he said, "if we have another corpse to find, *I'm* going to get a shower, a shave and some breakfast."

"Good idea," Perkins said. "Gosh, look at it rain. . . . Sure is going to be good fishing this year."

CHAPTER VII

NINE O'CLOCK Saturday morning found the rain still falling steadily, not with the torrential downpour which had characterized the early morning hours, but in a cold, steady, dispiriting drizzle. Doug Selby shook rain drops from his coat, hung it on the hat tree in his office and sought solace in a pipe of fragrant tobacco. His secretary brought him the mail, and Selby waved her aside when she made inquiry about dictation.

For some fifteen or twenty minutes he sat at his desk, eyes staring fixedly into space, the warm bowl of his pipe nestling in the palm of his hand, giving him a certain sense of companionship, the little clouds of fragrant smoke which he ejected from time to time helping him in his concentration. His secretary quietly entered the room and said, "Sylvia Martin from *The Clarion*."

"Show her in," Selby said.

Sylvia Martin entered the office with the breezy informality of one who is certain of her ground. Slightly younger than the district attorney, she presented to the world an exterior of trimly tailored figure, laughing reddish-brown eyes which matched her hair, a saucy, upturned nose, and lips which were always ready to smile. Only those who were privileged to know her intimately appreciated that back of her quick wit and facetious comments was a chain-lightning mind and a burning ambition to succeed in her profession. "Hi, Doug!" she said.

He returned her greeting, swung around to face her as she dropped into a chair. She surveyed his pipe with approval. "The old sleuth himself," she said.

He grinned. "What can I do for *The Clarion* this morning?"

"What's the low-down on the affair at the Keystone Auto Camp, Doug?" she asked.

Selby tapped ashes from the bowl of his pipe, then thrust moist, fragrant tobacco into the warm bowl and lit up again. "I was called," he said, "somewhere around four o'clock this morning by . . ."

"Not that," she interrupted. "I have all that from the sheriff and coroner's office. What I want is the low-down."

"You mean the facts that . . ."

"Not facts," she said, "conclusions. What do you make of it, Doug?"

"Frankly," he told her, "I don't know."

"Otto Larkin," she said, "the chief of police, is, of course, strong for *The Blade*. I have an idea *The Blade* will play it up in their evening edition with a lot of human interest. I'd like some new developments for our morning edition."

"Well," he told her, "perhaps there'll be some new developments."

"My city editor," she grinned at him, "doesn't like perhapses, so suppose we make the new developments now."

"Along what line?" he asked.

"Oh, on the human interest angle. How about commenting on the fact that the son of one of the city's most prominent men was participating in that game?"

"You can use your own judgment about that."

"Was Stapleton really there?"

"Yes."

"And is it true that you picked up an I O U of his for one hundred dollars?"

Selby grinned. "You must have got up before breakfast this morning, Sylvia."

"Oh, I get around," she admitted. "How about it, Doug?" He nodded his head. "That Stapleton business is news," she said. "I don't know if the editor will run it. Charles DeWitt Stapleton just about runs this town. And, if you ask me, I think it's a shame. But just because he's president of the beet sugar factory, a lot of people will kowtow to him—and how he eats it up. . . . Are you going to charge Triggs with gambling, Doug?"

"I don't know yet," he told her.

"Well, if you don't prosecute, my paper probably won't publish anything about George Stapleton. Why wouldn't you prosecute, Doug—on account of Inez?"

He felt himself flushing. "No," he said shortly.

"You be careful," she cautioned. "Charles DeWitt Stapleton would be a bad man to have as an enemy, and he'll crack the whip. . . . Oh, Doug, I wish you wouldn't let them pull the wool over your eyes—the Stapletons, I mean."

He said doggedly, "Triggs is going to stop letting young people gamble out there. I don't care what influence is brought to bear on me, or by whom."

"Well," she said, "you can't blame Triggs. Lots of his patronage comes from the young bloods of the town. The older people who want to play around go to Los Angeles, get rooms in the hotels and cut loose with their particular brand of adult wickedness. The youngsters have to be home some time before morning. The girls' mothers won't stand for unchaperoned trips to the city. So they go out to the road houses and dance and have a few drinks and park and pet on the way home. Such, in case you don't know it, Mr. District Attorney, are the facts of life as it is lived in a thriving rural community."

"I know all about it," he told her, grinning.

"Now George Stapleton is a pretty snappy number," she said. "*He's* one of the younger generation who hangs around the night clubs of Los Angeles and San Diego quite a bit."

"I know it," Selby told her. "I guess Triggs is acting on the theory it's better to keep the Stapleton money in the community."

She laughed lightly. "You probably mean that as a joke, Doug, but you'd be surprised at how many of the merchants feel that's just what Triggs is doing. If you start closing him up you'll find there's quite a bit of sympathy for him in town. He's shrewd enough to buy all of his supplies locally for cash, and he makes donations to civic causes, helps out the Chamber of Commerce and all that stuff."

Selby said, "I know. But he's going to quit importing professional gamblers."

"Okay," she said, "that's settled then. How about the low-down on this Keystone Auto Camp business?"

"What low-down do you want?"

"First," she said, "I want an interview with the girls."

"I'm sorry," he told her, "but that's out."

"Why's it out?"

"Those girls were on the level," Selby told her. "But a lot of newspaper readers won't believe it. Those girls live in a rural community and the newspapers will . . ."

"Look here, Doug Selby, do you mean to tell me that you're not going to give *me* the names and addresses of those girls?"

"I'm not."

"Now that," she said indignantly, "shows just how much good it does a newspaper to play ball with you!"

"What do you mean?"

"All during the election," she said, "*The Clarion* was for you. *The Blade* was plugging for Sam Roper, who naturally wanted to be re-elected. Now then, since you're elected, the least we can expect is that you'll give us an inside track with the news. *The Blade* will interview those two girls."

"No, it won't," he said. "Rex Brandon looks at it the way I do."

She laughed sarcastically and said, "Oh, is that so? And what is Otto Larkin, the chief of police, going to do?"

"He's going to co-operate," Selby said. "It's entirely out of his jurisdiction."

"You may think it's out of his jurisdiction, but I'll bet

he's already given all the dope to *The Blade*, including the names and addresses of those girls. Now just wait and see what happens. *The Blade* will come out to-night with an editorial roasting you for your failure to disclose the names. They'll keep that up for a couple of days and then they'll claim they've found the girls through the ingenuity of a *Blade* reporter. And then when they *do* interview them, they'll try to pin something on them just to make you look cheap. The result of your efforts to keep the girls out of it will only be to get them into it that much deeper."

"That may be," Selby conceded, "but in any event *I'm* going to *try* to keep them out of it."

Her eyes narrowed as she regarded him in thoughtful appraisal. "Is young Stapleton mixed up in it?" she asked.

"I don't know."

"If he is, it's going to be embarrassing. You've been seen quite a number of times with Inez. The Roper crowd will make political capital of it. They won't come out in the open, but there'll be little whispered conferences on the corners of Main Street, and rumors will run around the town like wildfire."

"What makes *you* think George Stapleton's involved?" Selby asked.

"Ross Blaine said that some of your questions indicated you thought he might have been the one the dead man was laying for. That's what I want to find out, Doug, what made you think he was mixed up in it?"

"I didn't," Selby said, "and I'm not certain that I do. But get this, Sylvia: There are one or two significant things about this which I think have been overlooked."

"What, for instance?"

"Did Harry Perkins show you all of the man's possessions?"

"Yes. They were in the lock-box. I looked through them, and of course Perkins extended the same courtesy to the *Blade* reporter. He's too shrewd a politician to play favorites so far as news is concerned. He dishes it out with a free hand."

"Were you impressed by anything strange about those possessions?"

"You mean the carpenter's pencil?"

"No," he said, "I mean the fact that he didn't have any keys."

"Well, Doug, he was a hitch-hiker. Hitch-hikers don't have homes, therefore . . ."

Selby interrupted her. "The door on the cabin was locked when the officers found the body. Rex Brandon opened it with a passkey."

"But surely, Doug, those locks don't amount to much. Any ordinary passkey will . . ."

"But this man didn't have a passkey," the district attorney interrupted. "That means someone was with him when he entered the place. That someone had a key, either the key to the cabin or a key which would fit the cabin. I'm inclined to the theory there were three people who entered the place, this hitch-hiker whom we found dead, and two others."

"On account of the whiskey glasses?" she asked.

He nodded and said, "Moreover, they must have entered the place some time before two o'clock in the morning because there was dust on the shoes of the dead man but no mud. It started to rain about two o'clock and has kept up a steady downpour ever since.

"Now then, let's suppose this hitch-hiker, Emil Watkins, and two companions entered the cabin together. They had a drink of whiskey. The two companions left and locked the door behind them. Watkins waited. He intended to kill someone. Obviously, therefore, that someone was going to come to the cabin, since it was manifestly impossible for Watkins to come to them."

"Could Watkins have been placed in there as a prisoner?" she asked. "Locked in and . . ."

He interrupted her to say, "Not a chance in a thousand. The windows could have been raised from the inside. Watkins could have stepped out through a window any time he wanted to. Or, he could have taken his gun and shot the lock off the door."

Selby's secretary opened the door and said, "Mr. Grace

from the Keystone Auto Camp is here and says it's very important that he see you at once."

Selby glanced meaningly at Sylvia Martin and said, "Tell him to come in."

Sylvia arose, as though to go. "Don't go, Sylvia," Selby said. "I'll give *The Clarion* a break."

The door opened, and Grace came bustling into the room, said, "Good morning, Selby," and paused when he saw Sylvia Martin. He said dubiously, "Good morning, Miss Martin. I didn't know you were here."

Selby said, "Miss Martin and I are having a very important conference. Of course, she *can* step out in the other office if you don't want to have her hear what you're going to say."

Grace said, "I *want* her to hear what I have to say."

"That makes it fine," Selby told him. "Sit down and tell me what it is. But first tell me where you were last night, or, rather, early this morning."

"I was in Los Angeles. My son arrived rather unexpectedly from the East."

"And you were with him?"

"That's right."

"What time did you leave your camp?" Selby asked.

"Around midnight," Grace said.

"Rather an unusual time to leave?" Selby asked.

Grace flushed. "I don't know what you're getting at, Selby," he said. "I'm running an honest business down there and I have a right to leave any time I want to. As a matter of fact, my son wired me he was taking the plane from Chicago which arrived at two o'clock in the morning, and I went down to meet him."

"Did you meet him?"

"No, he wasn't on the plane. There'd been a mix-up in sending the telegrams. Someone made a mistake. It turned out that he'd arrived on the plane which got into Los Angeles at ten o'clock and when I wasn't there to meet him he went to a hotel. When he didn't show up on the two o'clock plane, I got the traffic office to make an investigation and they found he'd been listed as a passenger on the earlier plane. So I rang the hotel where he usually stays and found he was registered there. But he wasn't in. I went to the hotel and he came in about three o'clock. We visited until five and then I went to a Turkish bath for two or three hours and came back here —in case it makes a damn bit of difference where I was or what I did."

"It's not that," Selby said, "but I thought it was rather unusual for a man to be running an auto camp and not be there and not have anyone in the office. We had to use a passkey in order to get into the cabin."

"I know all about it," Grace said, "and the sheriff went back and used a passkey to get into the office and took the register. I don't think you fellows had any business doing that."

"We'd have explained the situation to you if you'd been available," Selby said. "You see, there was some chance this man Watkins had got into the wrong cabin by mistake. We couldn't find any reason why he'd want to kill either of the occupants of that cabin, so we thought we'd check up on the occupants of some of the other cabins."

"All right, I'm not kicking so much about that," Grace said, "as about something else. I want you to hear what I have to say."

"Go ahead," Selby invited. "What's on your mind?"

"It's just this," Grace said. "I've been having a dispute with the gas people about my gas bills. I claimed the cabins wouldn't use as much gas as they claimed I've been using. So we made a test on this one cabin. We put in a special gas meter and I took daily readings. I took a reading on the meter in that cabin after the tenants moved out yesterday. It had been a cold night and there'd been a lot of gas used. I was checking up on it pretty carefully. So, after I got back from Los Angeles this morning and found out about this man having been found dead, I realized I could check up on the gas meter and tell just how long that gas stove had been burning. So I read the gas meter, and I don't believe it had been burning more than an hour and a half at the outside."

Selby said thoughtfully, "You're certain of your figures?"

"Yes."

"Then," Selby said, glancing at Sylvia Martin, "by figuring the time when Rex Brandon shut off the gas, we should be able to tell at approximately what time this man entered the cabin."

"That's one of the things I was getting at," Grace said.

"That," Selby told him, "might be rather important. Of course, we don't know that he turned the gas heater on as soon as he got into the cabin."

"Well, you can bet he didn't stay there very long without having it on," Grace said. "Those cabins get good and cold this sort of weather."

"Well," Selby told him, "I'm tied up here for part of the day. Suppose I come down there at three-thirty. You keep the cabin locked and make sure the stove and gas meter aren't tampered with."

"All right," Grace said. "Now here's something else: I want you folks to cut out this business of saying I had defective equipment down there."

"I haven't *said* it," Selby observed, "but I do think your gas heater was badly out of adjustment."

Grace flushed. "Now you look here, Doug Selby, a man wouldn't want to have that stove going full blast more than half an hour. That would heat a room so it was like an oven. Now, when you come down there to test that gas meter this afternoon, I want the privilege of locking myself in that room and staying half an hour. That'll show whether the equipment's defective or not. Of course, if a man's a damn fool and leaves any gas stove going full blast until the room gets as hot as a bake oven, he's going to smother one way or another. But I want an opportunity to prove that my equipment ain't defective, and I want to do it before the coroner's jury takes up the case."

"Well," Selby said, "personally I don't see that it's going to prove anything, but if you want to stay in that room for half an hour, it's all right with me."

Grace said, "And I want to be called as a witness at the inquest, and I want you to be a witness to show that I was in there for half an hour."

"Doubtless that could be arranged," Selby said with a smile.

"And," Grace went on, turning to Sylvia Martin, "I want the newspapers to publish what I'm going to do."

"Don't worry," she told him, "I'll be down there and you'll read all about it in the papers."

Grace nodded, turned on his heel, started toward the door, then swung back to say, "You know, Selby, Otto Larkin and I are great friends. He was for Roper the last election so I tagged along for Roper, but there wasn't anything personal against you in it. Now you're elected, I'm willing to let bygones be bygones if you are."

"I am," Selby said, grinning.

"That's all right then."

Sylvia Martin, with some folded news print paper on her knee, and a 6-B pencil poised over it, said to Grace, "Wait a minute, Mr. Grace, you can't get away without giving me some news for my column of comings and goings. Which son was it you met in Los Angeles, Talbot?"

"That's right, Talbot."

"What's he doing now?"

"He's sales manager for a concern back in Chicago."

"How long's it been since you've seen him?"

"Five years, going on to six," Grace said. "No, maybe it's longer than that. Maybe it's six, going on to seven. I can't remember. We had an argument and he left home—but that's all patched up now—I don't want anything said about that. Just say that James Grace went to Los Angeles to meet his son who's an executive in an important Eastern manufacturing company, and let it go at that. . . . No, wait a minute, you might say that he came out by airplane. That shows how important his job is."

"When's he going back?" Selby asked.

"He's already gone back. Left at nine o'clock this morning. That is, he flew from here up to San Francisco.

He stays there until Monday night. Then he flies to Seattle and from Seattle he goes back to Chicago. I'm telling you, Madison City had ought to be proud of Talbot Grace. He's making a name for himself back East, and there ain't many people in this town that come anywheres near making the salary Talbot does. . . . All right, Selby, I'll see you at three-thirty this afternoon."

He strode toward the door, jerked it open, and slammed it shut behind him. Sylvia looked over at the district attorney with a grin. "Sorry to have to delay matters while I get my personals, but it's all grist that comes to my mill."

Selby's eyes were narrowed into thoughtful slits. "If we can find out exactly when Emil Watkins entered that cabin, it may mean a lot."

She nodded, folded her paper and thrust it in her purse. "Okay, Doug, I'll see you at three-thirty down at the Keystone Auto Camp—and then you're going to tell me all about this dead man."

"What do you mean, all about him?" Selby asked.

She laughed, "Don't think I'm a fool, Doug Selby. I know your method of working on a case. You're going to dig into this man's life with a microscope. You're having his finger-prints checked, photographs of him taken, and I suppose you're having the Los Angeles police check up on all the carpenters by the name of Watkins."

Selby grinned and said, "Well, to tell you the truth, I am doing something like that. The Los Angeles police are getting in touch with the Carpenters' Union."

"How about finger-prints on the whiskey glasses, Doug?"

"There were prints on them," Selby said, "but they're too badly smudged to be of any value. There's a price mark on the whiskey bottle and I'm checking up with all the liquor dealers in the county to see if they sold the whiskey. By the time I see you this afternoon I'll have photostatic copies of that price mark. And, incidentally, Sylvia, I'm having those girls carefully checked on, up one side and down the other. If they're on the square,

I'm going to protect them. If there's anything off-color in their pasts, I'm going to take that fact into consideration."

"In case you decide to prosecute Triggs," she said, "let me know. I'm interested in seeing what Charles De-Witt Stapleton has to say about his wayward son."

"I suppose you'll be interviewing him on his arrival?" Selby inquired.

"Oh, of course. That's one of the little courtesies he expects when he returns to Madison City. We'll ask him all about business conditions in the East, what he thinks about the war situations in various parts of the world, his opinion about the stock market, and get his comments on the 1940 political possibilities. He'll look very grave and serious and answer all the questions we ask. We'll have a photograph of him being interviewed. . . . And you'd be surprised at how our readers eat that stuff up. Gosh, Doug, why is it they think a fellow citizen who's been transacting business in New York can come back and predict with unfailing accuracy what Mussolini will do next?"

Selby grinned. "I'll bite. Why is it?"

"Darned if I know," she told him. "Why don't you go to New York and come back and give us an interview?"

Selby said, "It might be a good idea, Sylvia. Would you be interested in knowing what's going to happen in the 1940 election?"

"To tell you the truth, Doug, I'm a darn sight more interested in knowing what's going to happen when *you* come up for election next time."

"So'm I," he admitted.

"All right, Doug. Three-thirty, then."

"Three-thirty," he told her. "Maybe earlier for lunch."

CHAPTER VIII

WITHIN ten minutes after Sylvia Martin had left the office, Inez Stapleton called the district attorney. "How about the tennis game, Doug?" she asked.

"In this weather?" Selby asked.

"There's an indoor court at the golf club. I've arranged for that."

Selby hesitated a moment and then said, "I'm sorry, Inez, but duty calls."

"Duty?" she asked, managing to put just the right amount of skepticism in her voice.

"I don't know whether you've heard about it, but a man was found dead in the Keystone Auto Camp. There are some rather mysterious circumstances surrounding his death."

Something in her voice put Selby on his guard. "As I remember it," she said, "we had a bargain and a definite date. I believe you mentioned that nothing short of a *murder* would keep you from keeping the appointment."

"Well," Selby told her, "I'm having to investigate to find out whether a murder has been committed."

"I thought the man died a natural death."

"*He* did," Selby said, "but after all, he may have killed the man he was after."

"I don't know too much about it," she said. "George said you took two friends of his to the coroner's office."

"When did you talk with George?" Selby asked.

"This morning."

Selby's eyes narrowed. "Would you mind telling me what time this morning?"

"Why, Doug?"

"I want to know. Was it immediately after George came home?"

"Yes," she said. "George woke me up coming in. I told him I thought it was altogether too late for him to be coming home. It was some time around half past five then."

Selby said, "Look here, Inez, I want to ask you a question."

"What?" she asked, and Selby could tell from the tone of her voice that she was very much on her guard.

"I want to know," Selby told her, "if you went up town this morning shortly before six o'clock."

"Good heavens, Doug! Why would I want to go up town?"

"And," Selby went on, "did you go into the All Night Drug Store and put in a call from the telephone booth?"

"Doug, you must be crazy! Why in the world would I . . . ?"

"That isn't answering my question," he told her.

"I'm not going to dignify any such question with an answer."

"That sounds evasive," Doug said.

Her voice grew indignant. "Doug Selby, don't think you can pull this district attorney stuff with me! Now, you had a date for tennis with me this afternoon. I called up to ask you if it was still on. You start in cross-examining me in your best lawyer manner. All I'm interested in knowing is whether we're going to play tennis."

Selby said obstinately, "This isn't an idle question, Inez. It's important. I want to know whether you went to the All Night Drug Store."

"And you," she told him, "can go to the devil!" Her voice rose in indignation. "I suppose," she said sarcastically, "I'll have to get a job on a newspaper if I want to see you at all!" And with that, Selby heard the bang of a receiver in his ear.

He hung up the telephone, refilled his pipe, and started pacing the office. He had been called shortly before six o'clock by some young woman who had been trying to disguise her voice. That young woman had told him a murder had actually been committed. Apparently, then, Emil Watkins had found his victim before he had gone to the cabin. Or, perhaps the man's program for vengeance called for the killing of more than one person.

This young woman had known that Selby would recognize her voice if he heard it. So she disguised it. Therefore, she must be someone whom Selby knew. Moreover, she had known that he was then at the coroner's office, since she had called him there. It certainly seemed absurd to think that Stapleton had confided something to his sister and she had left the house and dashed up to a pay station to put in a call to him. And yet it was a possibility. Something in the tone of her voice. Something in . . .

He heard Rex Brandon's unmistakable step in the corridor, the tapping of knuckles on the door. Selby opened the door. The sheriff walked in, dropped into a chair and said, "Trying to walk out a solution of the problem, Doug?" Selby nodded.

"I've done a little checking," Brandon said. "The numbers on that gun, for one thing. The gun was stolen a couple of months ago from a man in San Diego. He reported the theft to the police. The police investigated. Quite a few things had been taken from his house, along with the gun. So it seems to be all aboveboard. Of course, this man Watkins needn't have been the thief. The thief could have pawned the gun somewhere and Watkins could have bought it any time within the last two months."

"Anything else?" Selby asked.

"I've investigated those two girls. I've done it in such a way there won't be any publicity. They're apparently square-shooters. One of them's secretary in a building and loan, the other's secretary to a physician."

"I suppose Monette Lambert is the physician's secretary," Selby said.

"How did you know?"

"From the way she kept her head. Emergencies don't seem to faze her in the least."

"Well, your guess is right," Brandon said. "The girls have pretty good reputations. The boys are okay too, only they're a little wild at times. Now, here's something I did on my own," Brandon said somewhat sheepishly. "I don't know whether I did right or not."

"What's that?" Selby asked.

"I kept thinking about that woman who talked with you on the telephone from the All Night Drug Store," Brandon said.

Selby, noticing the expression on the sheriff's face, became instantly wary. "So what?" he asked.

"Well, look at it from this angle," Brandon said. "You said the girl who called you was evidently disguising her

71

voice, probably by holding something in her mouth. That meant that she was afraid you'd recognize her voice. That means you'd heard her talk somewhere before. Now then, she knew you were at the coroner's office. There weren't very many people who knew that."

Selby felt a strange feeling of apprehension gripping him. "Go ahead, Rex," he said to the sheriff. "What did you do?"

"Well," Brandon said, "it *could* have been either one of the two secretaries who were staying at the cabin. Or it could have been the hostess out at the road house. Those three girls knew you were going to the coroner's office. I can't figure anyone else did."

Selby felt an unaccountable surge of relief. "Go ahead, Rex. What did you do?"

"Well," Brandon said, "somehow I couldn't seem to warm up to the idea of those secretaries trying to tip you off in a telephone call, but I kept getting suspicious about that hostess, so I went out there and saw her."

"Why didn't you take me along, Rex?" Selby asked.

"I figured you're too young and impressionable and she's too good-looking," Brandon said.

"Did you accuse her of being the one who put in the call, Rex?"

"I did better than that, Doug. I even went so far as to tell her that the clerk in the drug store had recognized her."

"What did she do then?"

"Promptly proceeded to have hysterics, ran up to her room, slammed the door and locked herself in."

"How long ago was that, Rex?"

"Right after I'd had breakfast."

Selby withheld comment. "Anything else?"

"Yes. Here's something: I've found out that the keys on all those cabins are interchangeable. In other words, the key to one cabin will open them all. People would carry keys away with them and never send them back. Grace was always fooling around with a locksmith, having duplicates made. So he got passkeys which worked on all of the locks and now when people carry away a key he doesn't have to worry. He just takes down another one, ties the number of the cabin to it and lets it go at that."

"All right," Selby told him, "what are you getting at?"

"Those three glasses," Brandon said. "You know, Doug, it isn't likely that the boys would have come back and had a drink with this guy. It's not exactly logical that they planted him in the cabin. But suppose the girls had some reason for wanting to put him in the cabin? They could have done it easy. Their key would open the boys' cabin. And if they put this man in there and then both had a drink with him, there'd have been three glasses."

"But why," Selby asked, "would these girls have wanted to plant the hitch-hiker in that cabin?"

"So he could wait for the boys."

"It doesn't sound logical," Selby said.

"The whole business doesn't sound logical," Brandon told him.

Selby resumed his pacing of the office, puffing meditatively at his pipe. After a few minutes, he said, "Grace was in here. He has an idea he can show just about what time the gas was turned on last night. He's been taking daily readings on his meters. He'll have a man from the gas company down there at half past three this afternoon. Better arrange to be down there and we'll see what we can find out."

"It might help a lot if we knew exactly what time that gas heater was turned on. The . . ."

The telephone rang. Selby picked up the receiver and his secretary said, "Mr. Cuttings is calling long distance from San Pedro."

"Put him on," Selby said. A moment later, he heard the click of a connection, and Cuttings' voice saying, "Yes . . . Hello."

"Hello, Cuttings. This is Mr. Selby. What is it?"

Cuttings said, "I don't know whether it's important, Mr. Selby, but I thought I'd let you know anyway. Someone used my car last night, or early this morning."

"How do you know?" Selby asked.

"On account of the gasoline. She's pretty heavy on gas. I thought for a while someone might be siphoning gas out of the tank so I put on a locked gasoline cap. She sure does burn the gas. . . . Well, anyway, I ran out of gas about half way to Los Angeles. It happened where I could coast into a service station. But there should have been enough gas in the tank to have taken me clean into the city."

Selby said, "Look here. It started to rain around two o'clock. You put your car in the shed before then."

"That's right. About half past twelve."

"Now then, when you took it out," Selby asked, "did you notice whether the car had been out in the rain?"

"Come to think of it, I don't think it had. . . . No, I'm quite sure it hadn't."

"Then whoever took your car must have taken it before it started to rain."

"That's right. It was taken before two o'clock."

"Any idea how far it was driven?"

"Judging from the place where I ran out of gas, I'd say it must have been driven around twenty or twenty-five miles, perhaps a little farther."

"By the way," Selby said, "about that whiskey bottle and the three glasses we found in the cabin, that whiskey didn't come out of your bag, did it?"

"No, sir."

"You're certain?"

"Absolutely."

"And didn't come out of Gleason's bag?"

"No, sir, we never saw that bottle of whiskey before, Mr. Selby. We haven't any idea how it got there. We were talking it over all the way down, and we, neither of us, know a single thing about the whiskey or the glasses."

"All right," Selby said, "I was just making sure. Now is there anything else you've thought of?"

"No, sir, not a thing. I thought I should report about the car being used. I thought it might be important. You'll find us here on the yacht in case you want us. I gave Sheriff Brandon our address. Has . . . Have . . . I mean . . . Are there any new developments? Do you know anything more about what happened?"

"No," Selby said casually, "I guess there's nothing very much to it, just a hitch-hiker who was a crank. He may have been looking for a place to spend the night. He saw it was getting ready to rain, so he broke into the cabin, thinking it was vacant."

"But," Cuttings pointed out, "our bags were there in plain sight. He must have known we'd be coming back."

"That's right," Selby admitted, "I hadn't thought of that. Well, anyway, the man's dead and there's nothing we can do about it. If he'd lived he'd probably have committed a murder, so it's just about as well, taken by and large. Thanks for calling, Cuttings."

"Yes, sir," Cuttings said, and hung up.

Selby dropped the receiver into place and turned to Brandon. "Someone used Cuttings' car and drove it about twenty miles. That was before it started to rain. I'm adopting the attitude with him that it's just a casual, everyday sort of tragedy. In other words, I want to give those boys plenty of rope and then see if they get tangled up."

Brandon nodded. Selby's secretary opened the door and said, "Mr. Triggs is in the outer office. He seems very excited and wants to see you at once."

Selby glanced at the sheriff, received a short nod by way of reply, and said, "Send Mr. Triggs in."

Triggs entered the office, his face without expression, but he paused for a moment in the doorway as he saw the sheriff. Then he nodded coolly and walked across to Selby's desk. "What is it, Triggs?" Selby asked.

"I came," Triggs said, "to make a complaint about Sheriff Brandon. I didn't know he was here. However, since he is here, he may as well know how I feel about it."

Selby warned Brandon to silence with a quick glance and said, "How you feel about what, Triggs?"

"About what Brandon did this morning."

"What did he do?"

"He came out to my place," Triggs said, "and woke everybody up pounding on the door."

"What time was that?" Selby inquired, once more flashing a glance at Brandon.

"Around eight o'clock."

"And who was there?"

"Needham, the broker, Carlo Handley, Madge Trent and my'self."

"You say. Needham's a broker?"

"Yes. A retired broker."

"And what's Handley's occupation? You didn't mention that."

Triggs' eyes glittered and he said, "I don't know what it is. If you want to know, why don't *you* ask him? So far as I'm concerned, he's a good customer. That's all I know. Unless a man volunteers some information when he's out at my place, I don't try to pry into his personal business."

"Not even when he spends the night under your roof?" Selby asked.

"That's the first time either one of them ever spent the night there. This morning was different. It was raining and after all the excitement out there, I told them I'd put them up if they wanted. Everyone had gone to bed and just got to sleep when Sheriff Brandon came out, made a lot of commotion, got me up and demanded to talk with Madge Trent. I wasn't going to call her, but she heard him asking for her, slipped on something, and came downstairs. The sheriff accused her of having gone up to the All Night Drug Store, called you at the coroner's office, and told you that a murder had already been committed and you weren't to have the wool pulled over your eyes by that penciled statement which was by the man's body, and a lot of stuff like that.

"That was bad enough. But then he went on and said that the clerk at the All Night Drug Store had positively identified Madge as the woman who went up and put in the telephone call. That didn't sound right to me. It sounded like a damn bluff. But Madge fell for it. She thought some fool clerk had hypnotized himself into believing he'd seen her and that she was going to have a lot of notoriety and publicity. Madge has a daughter and

she didn't want this kid to see her mother's picture in the papers. Madge was all upset because of what
had taken place earlier. And when this other thing hit
her, on top of a loss of sleep and general nervousness, she
had hysterics. She dashed up and locked herself in her
bedroom.

"Now then, I went right down and hunted up the
clerk who was on duty at the All Night Drug Store and
asked him about it and he said that he absolutely could
not identify the woman who put in that call; he hadn't
seen her clearly enough. He thought she'd driven up with
some man, but he couldn't even be certain of that. All he
knows is that someone was waiting outside in an automobile and honked the horn and then the girl sprinted from
the telephone booth."

"And what happened to Miss Trent?" Selby asked.
"Is she ill? Perhaps if there's any question about what
happened, we'd better have a physician look her over."

"You won't be able to have a physician look her over,"
Triggs said with bitterness in his voice.

"Why not?" Selby asked.

"She isn't there."

"Where is she?"

"I don't know. She locked herself in her room and had
hysterics. You could hear her laughing and crying and
screaming all over the place. I went to her door and tried
to quiet her down. She quit screaming, but I could hear
her sobbing. You evidently don't know what it means to
her. She has this little girl she's putting through school,
and she'd kill herself before she'd subject that girl to all
the notoriety which would result from having her mother
involved in a criminal case. The people who have the girl
don't know what Madge does for a living, and she don't
want 'em to know."

Selby said, "Well, you can't blame Sheriff Brandon because her nerves were upset."

"I blame Sheriff Brandon for lying to her about what
that man in the drug store said."

"Perhaps you misunderstood Sheriff Brandon," Selby
said.

Triggs laughed sarcastically and said, "That line won't get anyone any place. Needham and Handley could hear every word that was said. It was daylight then and not raining so hard. They got up and dressed and drove back to Los Angeles. They said they'd as soon drive back as try to sleep in a place where officers kept busting in and girls kept screaming."

"Did they go together?" Selby asked.

"No. Handley went first. Needham hung around for a few minutes, being more polite about it. Handley was sore as hell, and showed it. I don't think either of them ever will come back."

"It may be just as well for you if Handley doesn't come back," Selby said significantly.

Irritation crept into Triggs' voice. "I'm not talking about Handley now," he said. "I'm talking about Brandon's high-handed methods and the false statements he made. He's made a nervous wreck out of Madge. Half an hour ago I went up to call her and tell her to take charge of the place because I was going to town. She didn't answer. I kept pounding on the door and still didn't get any answer. I tried it and it was locked. I thought perhaps she might have taken poison or something, so I used a duplicate key and got the door open. She was gone. The door was locked from the inside. She'd evidently climbed out of the window, dropped down to the roof and beat it."

"Why didn't she leave by the door?"

"She was hysterical."

"She doesn't owe you any money, does she?"

"No."

"Do you owe her any?"

"Yes, about two weeks' wages."

"Did anyone see her go?"

"No."

"How do you know she went out through the window?"

"The window was open. From that window, you can step out on the roof of one of the wings, then it's an easy drop down to the ground. The door was locked from the inside."

"Does she have an automobile?"

"No."

"What time did you go to bed?"

"I don't know, around six o'clock I guess."

"Did Madge Trent leave the place to come up town?" Selby asked.

"No, she didn't," Triggs said belligerently. "She stayed right there all the time."

"You're certain of that?"

"Yes."

"Then you were there all the time yourself?"

"That's right."

"Just what," Selby asked, "did you want us to do?"

Triggs said, "I wanted to talk with you. I thought I could count on *you* to be fair."

"Go ahead and talk," Selby said.

"I can, of course, sue Sheriff Brandon for damages—that is, Madge Trent can. But I don't want to do that. I want to find Madge Trent. She's out of her head, wandering around in the rain somewhere. I can't find her. I want you people to pick her up."

Selby said, "You can count on our co-operation as far as that's concerned, Triggs."

"And after you find her," Triggs said, emotion making his voice quaver, "for God's sake, show some compassion, show some decency in the way you treat her. She's a girl who has a kid to support and she's on her own. What's more, she's on the square. You keep on the way you're doing, and you'll have her completely crazy—if she isn't crazy now."

Brandon fidgeted uneasily. "I'm sorry, Triggs," he said, "if I . . ."

"Never mind, Sheriff," Selby interrupted. "I think you'd better let me handle it. We'll see if we can pick her up. You don't know what time she left, Triggs?"

"No."

"Did she take anything with her?"

"Apparently not."

"We'll try and find her," Selby promised.

"And after that you'll show some consideration in the way you treat her?" Triggs asked.

"You can rest assured we won't do anything that's going to subject her to any undue nervous strain," Selby said.

Triggs hesitated a moment, then said, "Please let me know as soon as you hear anything about her. Just get her located. I'll go out and bring her back. The county won't be put to any expense." He walked across the office and out of the door without once turning back.

Brandon's voice showed that he was uneasy. "I suppose I did go too far with her," he said. "Gosh, I wouldn't have hurt her for anything. I thought that hysterical business was just put on for effect."

"She probably went out to the highway and hitchhiked to Los Angeles," Selby said. "I'm not so certain the hysterics weren't assumed, Rex."

"What do you mean?" Brandon asked.

"You went out there," Selby said slowly, "and accused her of having gone into the All Night Drug Store and telephoned to me. Triggs heard you. She ran up to her room, locked herself in and had hysterics. Then she quieted down and commenced to cry. . . . Suppose she *had* gone up to the drug store and telephoned me; and suppose the man who drove her up was someone who hadn't figured in the case. You told her in front of Triggs that the man at the drug store could identify her as the one who'd put in the call. Suppose that made her afraid, not of you, but of Triggs. So she ran up to her room and went through the motions of having hysterics. When she had a chance, she went out of the window to the roof and then down to the ground. Somehow, Rex, it sounds more to me as though she were running away from Triggs than from you. Now then, Triggs comes in and seems very much concerned. He wants us to use all of the facilities at our command to locate her, and then *he* wants to be notified when we've located *her*."

"You mean he wants us to play bird dog for him?"

"That's right," Selby said. "Notice, he says that if we'll let him know as soon as we get any clew, he'll run down the clew himself."

Brandon nodded. "Maybe you're right, Doug. . . . Gosh, I hope I didn't seriously upset her."

"Forget it," Selby told him. "Whatever's been done has been done. Suppose you broadcast a description and see if we can get a line on her."

CHAPTER IX

SELBY met Sylvia Martin for lunch. They talked casually for a few minutes, then Selby asked, "What's new, Sylvia?"

"Nothing at my end," she said. "What do you know that's new?"

He told her about Triggs and the hysterical hostess. Sylvia frowned thoughtfully. "It doesn't sound right, Doug," she said.

"Why not?" Selby asked.

"Did you ever have hysterics?" she inquired. Selby laughed. "You know, Doug, what I'm getting at is that the things which leave you so awfully upset are the things that you can't have hysterics over. Having hysterics is sort of a safety valve. It lets off steam and keeps the boiler from blowing up."

"So what?" Selby asked.

"If she really had hysterics and laughed and screamed and cried, and then settled down to steady sobbing, her nerves would have been pretty much rested. Ordinarily, she'd have gone to sleep and slept for a while. She's a pretty level-headed girl with a great deal of poise. I suppose she has plenty to worry about, but as far as that's concerned, we all do."

"Well," Selby told her, "we'll see what Grace has to show us down at the cabin and then we'll go take a look down at the Palm Thatch and see what we can find."

"Anything else new?" she asked.

He took a couple of photostatic prints from his brief case. "These are enlargements of the cost and selling price which was written on the label of that whiskey bottle," he said.

"One of these for me?" she asked.

Selby nodded. "I wish you'd publish it."

"How about *The Blade?* Will it beat us to it?"

"I don't think so," Selby said. "I doubt if they can get it in time. We just received the photographs a few minutes ago."

Sylvia studied the photographic enlargement showing a section of the printing on the label and the penciled figures. She opened her brief case, slipped the photograph inside and was silent for several seconds. The waitress brought dessert. Sylvia played with hers, finally pushed it away and looked up at him. "Doug," she said, "I'm going to shoot square with you." He raised his eyebrows. "I think I know where that whiskey came from," she said. "Now, I know it's poor business for me to tell you. If you do anything about it now *The Blade* will find out about it and may even beat us to it. I should sit tight until after *The Blade* goes to press. But I'm anxious to have you clear this thing up."

"Go ahead," Selby told her, "I'll protect you on the news angle any way that I can, Sylvia."

"I know you will, Doug. . . . I hate to let loose of the information, though. My newspaper instinct tells me to sew it up."

"Of course," Selby said, "the sheriff's office will cover all the liquor stores as a matter of routine assignment, and if any of them recognize the cost mark . . ."

"They won't," she told him. "That cost mark is from a big drug store in Santa Delbara."

"You're certain?"

"Virtually certain, Doug. I buy facial creams there. It's a big drug store. . . . I think I recognize the figures. That five, with the long horizontal stroke, is just the same as the one on my foundation cream, and that cost mark, SEO, has an S that's made with straight lines.

. . . I'm certain that's where this whiskey came from."

Selby caught the eye of the waitress and motioned for the check. "Come on," he said, "we're going to make a sprint to Santa Delbara."

Selby led her to his car. The rain had ceased. The wind had shifted more to the west, and was increasing in velocity. Occasional patches of blue sky showed through the rifts in the clouds. Selby drove rapidly. As the roads dried off, he sent the needle of the speedometer quivering upward. It was nearing one-forty-five when Selby found a parking place in front of an imposing drug store which had a display of liquors in the window. The west wind, blowing in from the ocean, was cold and raw. But the danger of frost was over. The rain clouds had been swept from the valley, to pile up in dark banks against the mountains. With Sylvia at his side, Selby entered the store and asked for the manager. He introduced himself, took the enlarged photograph from his brief case and said, "I'm trying to locate this cost mark."

The manager glanced at the photograph and said, "Yes, this is our cost mark."

"It was on a bottle of whiskey," Selby told him. "I'd like, if possible, to find out everything we can about that sale of whiskey. I suppose it's asking too much to expect you to remember it, but perhaps if you could let us talk with your clerks. . . ."

"I think," the manager told him, "it will be easier than you expect. I happen to remember something about this myself. This is a very excellent grade of whiskey. We handled it in small lots for some of our exclusive trade. Then we received notice of a very sharp price increase, which I thought put it out of line with competitive merchandise, and we decided to discontinue it. I fixed a closing price to dispose of all of our stock, because, under our inventory system, it's a nuisance to be handling stock which we aren't going to replace. I remember we had a case of a dozen bottles, and I believe they were all sold to one purchaser. Just a moment, please."

The manager stepped into the back of the store, to return in a few moments with a rather surprised-looking clerk who regarded Selby with apprehensive eyes.

"This clerk can tell you all about it," the manager said.

"Of course, if that's just an isolated sale of a bottle, I can't tell much about it," the clerk explained apologetically. "That's the same cost price we've had on those goods for a year. But I remember we closed it out at a special price, and a young woman from Madison City bought the last twelve bottles as a birthday present for her father."

Selby involuntarily stiffened. "The name?" he asked, and his voice sounded strained even to his own ears.

"It was Stapleton," the clerk said. "Miss Inez Stapleton was the one who made the purchase. She comes in and buys quite a bit of stuff here, stuff that isn't carried in Madison City. And when the order came to close out this stock of whiskey, I was telling her about what a good value it was and . . . You see, she was in looking for something for her father's birthday. . . . I hope it's all right, sir."

"It's quite all right," Selby said. "How long ago was this shipment sent?"

"About six weeks ago."

"And you haven't handled this whiskey after that?"

The manager said, "I can answer that question. That last sale closed out our entire stock."

Selby said, "Thank you very much," and was grateful for the fact that Sylvia Martin did not once look at him as they turned and left the store side by side.

Not until they were back in the privacy of Selby's automobile and headed toward Madison City did she look up at him and say, "Well?"

"I don't know, Sylvia," Selby said thoughtfully.

"Do you think Inez knows anything about it?"

"No!"

"Well, you don't need to be so savage about it."   ·

"I wasn't savage about it," he said, his eyes fastened on the road, "I was merely answering your question."

"With rather a short monosyllable," she pointed out.

"Why are you so positive she doesn't know anything about it?"

"In the first place," Selby said, "she bought the whiskey for a birthday present. There were a dozen bottles in the case. She would have given her father the whole case. She wouldn't have given him ten bottles or eleven bottles or nine bottles. She'd have either given him twelve bottles, or none."

"That sounds logical," Sylvia Martin said, "so now we've traced the whiskey to Charles DeWitt Stapleton—I presume that means that he gave a bottle to George."

"And George might have given it to Cuttings or Gleason," Selby said. "But somehow, I don't think he did."

Sylvia Martin looked at her watch. "Charles DeWitt Stapleton is due to arrive at Madison City on the three o'clock train. If you step on it, you can be there and interview him when he arrives."

"I don't want to interview him when he arrives."

"Too hot to handle, Doug?" she asked.

"No," he told her, "but it has to be handled tactfully. It's a cinch Charles DeWitt Stapleton can't be mixed up in this thing."

Sylvia's silence indicated that she failed to share Selby's assurance. Selby went on, justifying his own position, "Stapleton's been in the East for almost a month. He couldn't have had any contact with this hitch-hiker."

Sylvia Martin said quietly, "Up until a couple of days ago we thought he was due yesterday afternoon, Doug. He laid over and took a later plane to Los Angeles. He's supposed to make train connections and arrive at three o'clock."

"He'll come from Los Angeles on the train?" Selby asked.

She laughed. "Of course he will. He could have had someone drive down to meet him in Los Angeles, but that's rather a private arrival. Stapleton likes the publicity of getting off the train and standing with just the right look of bored amusement while newspaper photographers gather round and people crane their necks out of the car windows."

"You evidently don't think much of our esteemed fellow townsman," Selby said.

"I think he's a stuffed shirt, if you ask me—big, pompous, dignified, and always patronizing everybody in town. It makes me sick the way they fall for it and lick his boots."

"After all," Selby told her, "the beet sugar company represents our biggest payroll."

She said bitterly, "I remember one night a new policeman picked up George Stapleton driving that big red car of his with about six drinks under his belt. He telephoned in for instructions. Chief Larkin went into a panic and told the officer to drive Stapleton home. Charles DeWitt Stapleton was furious. He called up Larkin and bawled him out, said George had had a couple of drinks, but was perfectly able to drive the car and Larkin cringed like a cur who's about to be whipped. I was in police headquarters at the time and heard the call come in. Larkin just crawled all over the officer. If I'd been in his shoes, I'd have telephoned the officer to have put handcuffs on George, brought him in, thrown him in jail and put a charge of reckless driving, and driving while intoxicated against him."

"Yes, you would," Selby said, grinning.

She looked up at him, with her mouth set in a firm, determined line and said, "You're damn right I would!"

CHAPTER X

SELBY dropped Sylvia Martin at the parking lot on Main Street where she had left her car. She still had five minutes to get to the station and meet Charles DeWitt Stapleton's train. "Remember, Doug," she said in her final admonition, "you're not to tell anyone about those whiskey bottles. That's my own individual scoop."

"Are you going to ask Stapleton about them?" he asked.

She laughed. "I'm going to ask Stapleton all about Mussolini, Hitler, the Oriental situation, the stock market, the Republican strategy for 1940, and the probable Democratic candidate," she said. "And he'll answer all my questions." She pressed a neatly shod foot on the starter of the light coupe and dashed out of the parking lot.

Selby drove to the courthouse. It was Saturday afternoon and the curb in front of the building, usually crowded with parked cars, was now almost deserted. Inez Stapleton's big cream-colored car was parked almost directly opposite the courthouse steps. Selby parked his own car and walked across to where Inez was seated behind the steering wheel. "Why aren't you down meeting your father?" he asked.

"Dad can wait," she said. "Been working, Doug?" He nodded. She glanced at him, then turned away. For a moment she stared thoughtfully through the windshield, then she turned back to face him. "Doug," she said, and there was suffering in her eyes, "the manager of the drug store in Santa Delbara where I do a good deal of my shopping telephoned me about fifteen minutes ago."

Selby frowned and said, "He would. I neglected to caution him about doing that."

Her eyes flashed. "Oh," she said, "so you weren't going to come to me, but were going to snoop around behind my back, is that it?"

"I don't know just how I intended to approach the situation, but I wanted to do it in my own way. I should have known, however, that the manager up there would have protected his customers."

"All right," she said, bitterly, "now let's have it out. Why are you interested in the liquor I bought my father for a birthday present?"

"Because," Selby said, "one of those bottles was on the dresser in the cabin where this dead hitch-hiker was found."

"It was not," she said positively.

"A bottle just like it," Selby said.

"Well, just because I buy a dozen bottles of liquor for

my father's birthday doesn't mean that we're responsible for the output of the entire distillery."

"It was a bottle purchased through that drug store, at Santa Delbara," Selby insisted.

"I don't care *where* it was purchased. Doug Selby, I think you're going crazy. Good Lord! After all, it's just some old hitch-hiker who crawled into a cabin and asphyxiated himself."

"He was waiting to kill someone," Selby said.

"Well, what if he was? My heavens, lots of people *want* to kill other people! He didn't *kill* anyone, did he?"

"No," the district attorney admitted, "but I want to find out whom he was after."

"Why?"

"It's part of the duties of my office."

"Well, I don't think so. The man actually didn't commit any crime. He met an accidental death. Why in the world do you want to go prying into a lot of things which are none of your business? After all, Doug, what difference does it make whom he intended to kill?"

"It may make a lot," he told her. "And, as far as that's concerned, why are *you* so interested in seeing that I *don't* pry into things?"

She blinked her eyes rapidly, turned away from him and was silent for a second or two. Then she said, without looking at him, "Because I like you, Doug. I value your friendship."

"What's that got to do with it?" he wanted to know with dogged persistence.

"Can't you see," she said, "what will happen if my father thinks . . . ? Oh, Doug, don't you know what Dad will do?"

"What will he do?" Selby asked.

"Plenty!" she said grimly. "He won't stand for this, Doug. He's a powerful man and he doesn't brook any interferences. You know Dad, Doug. He could crush you like . . . well anyway, he won't stand for your interference."

"I'm not interfering," Selby said calmly. "I want to know about that whiskey bottle. It's evidence in a case."

"What sort of a case?" she asked, and then went on to answer her own question, "Just a case of a bum who crawled in out of the rain and died."

"We won't go over that again," Selby told her.

"Doug, won't you *please* listen to reason?"

Doug said, "Look here, Inez, I'm *not* being unreasonable about this thing. That whiskey bottle was down at the cabin. I want to know where it came from. The occupants of the cabin say they've never seen it before. I had an opportunity to trace it. I went up to Santa Delbara to trace the purchase. That's *all* I've done."

"But you're intending to carry it farther. You're intending to question George and intending to talk with Father about it, aren't you?"

"I don't know," Selby said.

"Well, *I* know, and I want to warn you, Doug. *Please, please*, don't mix in it any farther."

"Why not?" he asked. "What are you trying to conceal?"

"I'm not trying to conceal anything," she said, her voice showing her exasperation; "I'm trying to save your political life. Doug, I want you to promise me you'll forget about that whiskey bottle. Good Lord, what difference does it make *what* the man was intending to do? What difference does it make . . . ?"

"Are you trying to protect George?" Selby interrupted her to ask.

She put her hand on his then and looked up in his eyes. "Doug," she said, "I give you my word of honor there's only one person I'm trying to protect, and that's you."

"You don't know that George had this bottle of whiskey?"

"To tell you the truth, Doug, I'm almost certain that he didn't. I gave Dad that dozen bottles and Dad likes the brand. Good grief, George has plenty of money to buy all the whiskey he wants for himself. I don't think he'd touch those bottles even if he could get at them. Dad locked them in his den at the house."

"Were you intending to tell him about the call which

came in from the Santa Delbara drug store?" Selby asked.

"No, of course not. And the reason I'm talking to you, Doug, is to get your promise that you won't mention it to him."

Selby shook his head obstinately. "I want you to tell him, Inez," he said. "I want you to tell him the entire circumstances."

"Why, Doug?"

"Because," Selby said, "that will save me the necessity of doing so. I want him to look in that closet and see if any of the whiskey bottles are missing."

"If they are, then what?"

"Then," Selby said, "I want to talk with George."

"And if they aren't, what?"

"If they aren't," he announced, puckering his fore-head in a thoughtful frown, "I suppose we'll have to assume the bottle was one which had been purchased some time ago by some transient and we'll have to let it go at that."

"Doug, please don't make me ask him."

"I want you to tell him," he told her. "Perhaps after all it's better to have it come up in this way."

"All right," she said, "I'll ask him. But I warn you, Doug, it's just going to result in antagonizing Dad and it won't lead you to anything. I'm absolutely, positively certain that that bottle of whiskey didn't come from our house. Dad keeps his liquor locked up. He likes that particular brand, and it's a brand that's hard to get. I know he took a couple of bottles with him in his trunk when he went East."

"Was that the first time you'd tried it," Selby asked, "when you bought the dozen bottles?"

"No. Dad bought some first. He liked it very much. That was why I bought the dozen bottles for his birth-day present. I wouldn't have bought that much unless I'd known he was going to like it."

"And you don't think George would have taken one of those bottles?"

"I know he wouldn't."

"Where is George?" Selby asked.

"He's home."

"How long has he been up?"

"He got up about nine o'clock—perhaps a little earlier. I don't know exactly what time it was. Ross Blaine came up and . . ."

"Go ahead," Selby said as she stopped.

"Well, he got up, that's all."

"Ross Blaine came up to see him?"

"What does that have to do with it? Good grief, Doug, why do you have to be so snoopy? What difference does it make *why* George got up?"

"Tell me about Ross Blaine," Selby said, his voice ominously level.

"Oh, well, if you must know, Mr. Inquisitor, Blaine came out, got George out of bed, held a conversation which I *didn't* eavesdrop on, and then drove away in George's new car."

"In George's car?"

"That's what I said."

"Where did he go?"

"I don't know. You see *I* don't go around prying into other people's business."

"Has he come back yet?"

"I don't know."

"You didn't ask George what Ross wanted, or where . . . ?"

"No! Stop it, Doug. I'm not going to be questioned this way. I know nothing whatever about George's affairs."

"Has he ever loaned anyone his car before?"

"Not that I know of. Please, Doug, leave George out of it."

"Have you told him anything about this whiskey?"

"No. He may be at the train, meeting Dad. Oh, Doug, why can't you be sensible? This man might have committed a murder if he'd lived. Again, he might not. What difference does it make? He's dead and that's all there is to it. I wish you'd let this thing drop."

"Well," Doug told her, "I'll think it over."

"Then I won't have to tell Dad about the manager of the drug store calling and . . ."

"No," he interrupted, "that's one thing I *do* want you to tell your father just as soon as you see him."

"Doug, I wish you weren't so dreadfully headstrong."

He smiled and said, "You're headstrong yourself. How about hanging up the phone in my ear this morning?"

"You had it coming to you."

"Why? Because I asked you if you'd been uptown this morning?"

"Because of the manner in which you asked it," she said.

"Well," Doug said, grinning, "now I'll come back to the subject. *Did* you go uptown this morning and . . ."

Her eyes filled with tears. Viciously, she jabbed her foot at the starter. "The friendship of a woman doesn't mean a d-d-d-damn thing to you, compared with that j-j-job of yours, does it?" she stormed. The engine pulsed into life. Inez slammed the car into reverse, straightened it out, and sent it into a screaming turn at the corner.

CHAPTER XI

IT WAS five minutes after three-thirty when Selby drove up to the Keystone Auto Camp. The cold west wind had swept the sky free of clouds, and was constantly increasing in volume, blowing away the threat of frost, yet chilling the body with its raw cold.

Sheriff Brandon was already there, and a moment after Selby drove up, Sylvia Martin drew up in her light coupe. She said cheerfully, "The gang's all here."

"How was the reception at the depot?" Selby asked.

"Up to par in every way," she said. "I can tell you all about the European situation. Business is getting ready to boom within sixty days. The stock market is going to climb to a new high. A bloc in Congress is going to attempt to denounce the Monroe Doctrine as a fatal weakness in our defense against European war. The Administration is planning on . . . Oh, what's the use? If I tell you all the news for the next two years, you'll cancel your subscription to *The Clarion* because you'll know everything that's going to happen in advance."

Selby laughed and said, "Come on. Grace and the gas man are waiting over here."

Grace made something of a ceremony of introducing the man from the gas company who was to read the meter. He pulled a pasteboard-backed notebook from his pocket and showed pencil figures of meter readings going through the past ten days. The man from the gas company explained the operation of the meter and how the dial could be read. Selby studied the penciled figures. "A lot more gas was used night before last than last night," he said.

"That's exactly what I'm telling you," Grace asserted. "The gas heater in there wasn't going very long."

"I notice a couple of erasures here," Selby told him, "one in the figures for yesterday."

"Well, yes," Grace admitted, "there *is* an erasure there, but it's just a mistake I made in copying a figure. . . . My God, you don't think I'd try to juggle figures, do you?"

"I was just asking for information," Selby said. "You're offering this book in evidence and I wanted to find out about the erasure."

"Well, you've found out about it," Grace said belligerently.

"Just what do you want *me* to do?" the man from the gas company asked. "Inside of fifteen minutes I can tell you just how much gas that stove is consuming and . . ."

"No," Grace told him, "we want you to stand right by that gas meter and we want to run that gas heater just as long as it was run last night, or this morning. Now then, I'm going to tell you fellows something. There have been a lot of cracks made about my equipment down here. I don't want a false impression to get around. I'm going in that cabin and close all the doors and windows. I'll turn that gas heater on full force and I'll convince you that it's absolutely safe to stay in there."

"If you're going to do that," Brandon told him, "you keep the shade up on the window and keep your eyes open. I'll be looking in at you, and the minute you close your eyes I'm coming through that door. Do you understand?"

"I won't close my eyes," Grace asserted. "That gas heater's absolutely safe."

"All right," Brandon said. "You understand the situation."

Selby said, "We'll walk around and take a look at the gas meter for ourselves and check the present reading."

"I've already checked it," the man from the gas company told him. "It's just the way it's written down there on the notebook."

"But you didn't check the figures on the preceding days?"

"No. I haven't been down here for four or five days, but I can tell you that the figures entered in there for four days ago are accurate, and the last figures in there are accurate, so that represents all of the gas which has gone through that meter in those four days."

"But you yourself don't know how the gas consumption was distributed during those four days—that is, except from these figures Grace has kept?"

"That's right."

"All right," Selby said, "let's go."

Grace entered the room, carefully closed the door and made certain the windows were tightly closed. He made signs to the officers indicating they were to consult their watches, then he struck a match, lit the gas heater, and turned on the gas full force.

Selby and Sylvia Martin stood together at one of the windows. Sylvia said, "Gosh, he's a glutton for punishment, but you have to hand it to him for having the courage of his convictions. Look at the way those flames hit the top of the heater, spread out and come up over the sides. I wouldn't stay in there if you'd give me the cabin."

"Me either," Selby agreed.

Grace sat on the edge of the bed, his eyes wide open, staring at the window.

"Look," Brandon announced, after four or five minutes, "his eyes are commencing to water. There's a lot of gas in there."

"How long does he intend to stick it out?" Sylvia asked.

"Just as long as the heater's going, I understand," Selby said. "However, Dr. Trueman said the man must have been dead for an hour or so before he was found. So Grace really should dock the meter an hour."

"Well, we'll keep a close watch on him," Brandon said.

Selby said, "Rex, I have an idea there's more to the disappearance of this girl from the Palm Thatch than appears on the surface."

"You mean the hostess?"

"Yes."

"I haven't been able to find out a thing so far," Brandon said. "I figured, if some motorist picked her up as a hitch-hiker and thought she was a bit hysterical or nervous, he'd report to the Los Angeles police, if she was going that way. So I've communicated with them and I've communicated with the police officers in all the towns between here and there. Then, I've done the same thing up the other way."

"I think she went to San Francisco," Selby said. "In fact, I have a pretty good lead which makes me think she did."

"Well, I've been in touch with San Francisco," Brandon observed.

"I wish you'd take a run up there, Rex."

"Take a run up to San Francisco?"

"Yes."

"Why?"

"I think you can find this girl up there."

"What makes you think that?"

Selby said, "A clew which I haven't time to discuss right now, but I have an idea you'll find she's gone to San Francisco and has been looking for work in some of the spots up there. I wish you'd take a run up, Rex. You can leave for Los Angeles just as soon as you finish here, take the train up and get one of the officers up there to drive you around to some of the different night spots."

"Do you think it's *that* important?" Brandon asked, frowning.

"Yes, I do," Selby told him.

Sylvia Martin turned to stare at Selby with narrowed eyes. She started to say something, then checked herself.

"After all," Brandon said, "this thing may be just a tempest in a teapot, Doug. This man wanted to kill somebody but he didn't do it."

"How do you know he didn't do it?" Selby asked.

"Well, for one thing, where's the body?" the sheriff inquired.

"If he did commit a murder," Selby said, "that's one of the things we want to find. After all, Rex, we don't know that this man only intended to kill one person. He may have intended to kill two. The one he was lying in wait for in the cabin may have been the second one.

"Now, here's something else, Rex: so far, we've acted on the assumption that this man was lying in wait for someone who was going to come back to this cabin; but there are two or three things in the evidence which indicate that this wasn't the case."

"What?" the sheriff asked.

"Well, for one thing, the lights were on. If he'd been waiting for the occupants of the cabin to come back, he wouldn't have left the lights on. The boys turned the lights off when they left. Naturally, if they'd returned and found the lights on, they'd have been suspicious. Now, notice that this man hadn't pulled the shade down all the way, but had left it up an inch or so at the bottom, far enough to enable the girls to look in and see his feet pushed out from under the bureau."

"Go ahead," Brandon said, "I'm listening."

Selby said, "That's inconsistent with the man's lying in wait for someone to come back to the cabin. If he'd been doing that, he'd have had the shade drawn all the way, and, furthermore, he'd have had the lights out. But suppose he was waiting for someone who was going to pass the cabin, going into the Keystone Auto Camp. Notice that this cabin is one next to the highway. The main driveway leads right past this window. The fact that the shade was raised an inch or two would indicate that Watkins had purposely left it that way so he could look out when the occasion demanded."

"He couldn't have looked out and seen anything with lights on in the cabin," the sheriff pointed out.

"No, but he could have switched out the lights very easily. If he'd been printing that note to pin on the body, he'd have needed the lights to see what he was doing."

"Then he wouldn't have been behind the bureau," Brandon said.

"I understand all that," Selby admitted. "But what I was saying was that the theory that Watkins had been lying in wait for the occupants of this cabin to return doesn't coincide with all the evidence. There's one other thing we haven't figured, and that is this man may have expected someone to enter the cabin other than the person who rented it."

"What are you getting at now?" Brandon asked.

Selby nodded toward James Grace, who was sitting inside of the room on the edge of the bed, his eyes streaming tears, perspiration beaded on his forehead. "Grace," Selby said, "had gone to Los Angeles, and was due to return some time well after midnight. Suppose this man had been waiting for Grace?"

"How do you figure that, Doug?"

"Just this," Selby said. "Suppose Grace *had* returned about three or four o'clock in the morning. He'd have seen lights on in one of the cabins. Naturally, he'd have stopped. The shade would have been raised an inch or two. Grace would have looked through to see what it was all about. Remember, Grace pays for the gas and lights. The fact that he's been having a dispute with the gas company over the gas shows he's checking up carefully on the utilities. He'd have looked through the window and seen the gas stove going full blast. Having a passkey to the cabin, seeing the lights all blazing and the gas stove going full tilt, what's more natural than that he'd have used his passkey to go in and shut off the stove."

Brandon nodded thoughtfully.

"Then," Selby said, "the man behind the dresser would have shot Grace, pinned the note on his body, slipped out of the door, and been on his way. We'd never have had the faintest inkling who he was, because we naturally wouldn't have connected up the hitch-hiker with the murder."

Brandon said, "By gosh, Doug, you *have* something there."

Selby said, "All right, keep it quiet, Rex. Let's give Grace lots of rope and see if he gets tangled up in it. Remember, he swore that he didn't know the hitch-hiker and had never seen him before."

"As far as that's concerned," Sylvia Martin interposed, "the hitch-hiker said in his note that the man he was going to kill didn't know who he was."

"That's right," Selby agreed.

Brandon said, "Gosh, Doug, let's take Jimmy Grace and shake him down. Let's give him a regular third-degree and find out . . ."

"I don't think you can do that," Selby said. "In the first place, I'm not so certain that Grace actually knows what Watkins had against him. All I've been doing so far is pointing out that the facts are inconsistent with Watkins lying in wait for the returning occupants of the cabin. And they're inconsistent with his having used the cabin as an ambush to shoot someone through the window. If he'd been doing that, he'd have had the window open an inch or two from the bottom and the lights off. But it *would* have been a perfectly baited trap to have enticed James Grace to his destruction, with the evidence all pointing to the fact that Cuttings and Gleason committed the crime."

"And, with the whiskey bottle and three glasses on the dresser," Brandon said, "it would look as though they'd all had a drink before Grace was killed." Selby nodded.

"Then there's no reason I should go to San Francisco," Brandon said.

"Yes, Rex, there is," Doug told him. "I'm coming to that. It's the most important reason of all. You remember Talbot Grace. He was due in Los Angeles on a plane. He took an earlier plane than he was supposed to have taken. No one knows where he was. He had ample opportunity to drive up to Madison City and back to Los Angeles. Now, Talbot Grace is in San Francisco today and will be over Sunday and Monday. He leaves Monday night for Seattle. I think it might be a fine idea for you to have a talk with Talbot Grace."

"Okay," Brandon said. "Just as soon as we finish here I'll drive into Los Angeles and catch the *Owl* north."

Grace got to his feet, mopped perspiration from his forehead, staggered unsteadily and fumbled his way toward the door. Brandon said excitedly, "Here he comes. He's all in," and ran from the window to the door. Selby and Sylvia followed. Brandon flung the door open. A blast of hot air, dead, lifeless, and enervating, poured from the room to strike their faces and assail their nostrils with a stinging sensation which brought water to their eyes. Grace, stumbling over the threshold, gasped his way into the fresh air and started to cough. He checked his coughing spell after a second or two, leaned up against the side of the cabin and said obstinately, "The gas heater's . . . all right . . . It just got too . . . damn hot in there. I'm all sweaty."

Brandon winked at Selby, put his arm under Grace's shoulders and said, "Feeling all right?"

"A little dizzy. . . . I guess my heart isn't as strong as it was. . . . It's just too hot in there, that's all. Like living in an oven. The gas heater's all right. No one would leave it on like that to heat up the place. . . . It ain't a question of the gas heater being too bad, it's a question of the gas heater being too damn good."

A yell came from the man who was watching the gas meter. Selby and Sylvia Martin ran around to him. "What is it?" they asked.

"Just thought I'd let you know," the man said. "Exactly one half the amount of gas has gone through this meter which went through it yesterday, according to Grace's figures."

Selby consulted his watch. "It's been exactly seventeen minutes," he said. The gas man nodded. Selby said, "Well, keep watching it." He took Sylvia Martin's arm and guided her toward the arched entrance of the Keystone Auto Camp, out of ear-shot of the man who was bending over the gas meter. "Well," he said slowly, "Grace has tangled himself up in his own story."

"How, Doug?"

"His own figures indicate a physical impossibility," Selby said. "Therefore, he must have tampered with those figures. He was so anxious to prove that his equipment wasn't defective that he overdid it. We know that the gas heater must have been going from before two o'clock in the morning until around twenty minutes to four. That's an hour and forty minutes."

"*How* do you know that?"

"They discovered the body about three-twenty. The girls dressed, ran to the telephone, and notified Larkin. Larkin got in touch with Rex Brandon. They got down here and shut the gas heater off about twenty minutes later. That makes it three-forty. Now then, Watkins had entered that cabin before it started to rain. There was dust on his shoes, but no mud. It started to rain at two o'clock."

"If you knew that, Doug," she said, "why did you let Grace fix up this test?"

"Because," Selby said, "I wanted to check on Grace. According to his figures, the gas heater was going for only thirty-four minutes. Now then, it was going twenty minutes after the body was discovered. If his figures are correct, Watkins could only have been in the cabin for fourteen minutes before the girl looked through the window and discovered his body. But that couldn't have happened, because Grace was in there for seventeen minutes just now without asphyxiating himself."

Sylvia Martin looked at Selby with suspicious eyes. "Doug, why are you so anxious to get rid of Rex Brandon? Why do you want him to go to San Francisco?"

"Because," Selby said, facing her, "I'm going to commit political suicide, and I don't want to drag Rex Brandon down with me."

"What are you going to do, Doug?" she asked.

Doug said, "I'm going to show Charles DeWitt Stapleton that as far as this county is concerned, *I'm* running the district attorney's office."

She flashed a quick glance at him, then, at what she saw in his eyes, pushed out her hand and said, "Put it there, Doug."

CHAPTER XII

SELBY drove to his apartment. The switchboard operator told him that Charles DeWitt Stapleton wished him to call just as soon as he came in.

Selby went to his room, placed the call, and heard Stapleton's close-clipped voice. "Hello, Selby. How are you?"

"Fine, thank you, Mr. Stapleton. Have a good trip?"

"A very busy trip," Stapleton said, tersely. "Selby, I have a personal favor I want to ask of you."

"What is it?" Selby asked, guardedly.

"I want to have a talk with you," Stapleton said. "I've just this minute returned from an extended Eastern trip. I find my desk piled high with correspondence and telegrams, and a dozen matters of the greatest importance require my immediate attention. Therefore, it's impossible for *me* to look *you* up. I wonder if you'd mind running down to my office for a few minutes."

"I'm working on a case," Selby said, "and . . ."

"It will only take a minute. I'm sure we can get things straightened out in a very short time."

"All right," Selby promised. "I'll come down. Where are you, at your factory office?"

"Yes. I'm in the sugar factory. There are some people waiting in the office, but I'll have my secretary show you in just as soon as you arrive."

"That will be in about five minutes," Selby told him.

Hê hung up the telephone, washed his hands and face, put on gloves, overcoat and hat, swung his car in a circle in the middle of the block, and gave it the gun. The Madison Beet Sugar Factory was some two miles out of town, an imposing structure which lay idle part of the year, but at other times was a hive of activity, with smoke belching from the towering stacks and steam sputtering from dozens of vents like some huge teakettle bubbling and boiling on the back of a wood stove. Selby entered the big yard, drove at once to the administration building and parked his car. He passed through the general offices, pushed open a door marked PRESIDENT and said to the secretary in the reception office, "I have an appointment . . ."

She was on her feet at once. "Yes, Mr. Selby," she said, "Mr. Stapleton will see you at once." She led the way past several persons who were sitting, waiting, held open an inner door, and Selby entered a sumptuously furnished private office.

Charles DeWitt Stapleton was the big man in Madison City. As president of the beet sugar company, he controlled the town's largest payroll, and nothing in his manner or bearing indicated that he was in anywise unconscious of his power and prestige. Tall, heavily fleshed, expansive and urbane, but with cold eyes and a hard mouth which lay in ambush beneath a close-clipped, gray mustache, he had the reputation of rushing business callers through his office with an average of less than three minutes to a call. "How are you, Selby?" he said, gripping the district attorney's hand. "You're looking fine, my boy! Responsibility seems to have agreed with you! Come over here and sit down . . . over here by the desk. . . . Have a cigar. . . . These are specially made for me in Havana."

With a lordly gesture of hospitality, Stapleton's plump, well-manicured hand flung back the lid of a humidor and extended the open receptacle toward Selby.

The aroma of fragrant Havana tobacco oozed out into the room.

Selby said, "No, thanks. I'm a confirmed pipe smoker, with an occasional cigarette."

Stapleton seemed somewhat disappointed. He held the cover of the humidor open for a second, then dropped it back into place and seated himself in the big swivel chair behind the desk. "Haven't seen you around at the house for some time, Selby," he said. "You and Inez used to play quite a bit of tennis and do some horseback riding. You aren't letting the cares of public office keep you from taking a proper amount of exercise, are you?"

"I think not," Selby told him. "Of course, I don't have as much time now as I did when I was practicing law."

"No, of course not. It's a very important position you hold—a *very* important position. But you must remember, Selby, that your first duty is to yourself. Your body is the machine which carries you through life . . . although I presume I'm a fine one to preach. It seems as though I'm on the go all the time, with conferences running far into the night. . . . However, you didn't come here to discuss *my* business, and I know that you're far too busy to take time out right now to discuss yours.

"I want to talk with you about my boy, George. I don't know how well you know him. I don't suppose he's been around the house much when you've been calling on Inez. The truth of the matter is that he's not much of a home boy. I don't suppose he's home one evening a month . . . but that's the way with boys these days. He's a good enough boy, but he's arrived at an age when his mother doesn't understand him. In fact, their lives have drifted apart. Mrs. Stapleton, as you are probably aware, has numerous social obligations. Her position as my wife . . . as well as her own charm," Stapleton added hastily, "make it incumbent upon her to spend much of her time away from home. My own business affairs keep me commuting between here and New York."

He paused long enough to let Selby appreciate the contrast between a man who was an integral part of

the nation's business, and a county official.
"Now, while I've been on this last trip," Stapleton
went on, "I find that George has been feeling his oats a
bit. Not only has he been exceeding his allowance, but
he's been giving I O Us and promissory notes and post-
dated checks. I understand he's been doing a bit of gambling." Selby nodded. "I also understand," Stapleton
went on, "that you know something about this."

"I caught him in a game early this morning," Selby
said. "That is, I happened to drop in on a game and your
son was playing."

"So I understand," Stapleton said. "Now, about this
Palm Thatch, Selby. My son tells me that he's met some
out of town people there, rather delightful people, but
I've gathered there's been a little something lacking with
their backgrounds." Selby nodded. "My boy tells me,"
Stapleton continued, "that you accused one of these men
of being a professional gambler. That started George
thinking. He'd always regarded this man as a business
man—an insurance executive who liked to play cards for
the excitement of it. But, since your accusation and the
manner in which this man acted when that accusation
was made, George began to see things differently. He
realized he'd been duped. He also realized that another
man, a retired broker named Needham, had been duped.
In fact, George . . ."

"How much has he dropped?" Selby asked abruptly.

Stapleton frowned. "Rather a considerable amount.
But it wasn't for the purpose of discussing that that I
wanted this chat with you, Selby."

"What did you want to discuss?" Selby asked.

"I feel that the Palm Thatch is a menace to the youth
of this community. I feel that it should be wiped out,
completely eradicated."

"They're going to quit gambling there," Selby said
grimly.

"That's fine," Stapleton agreed, "and when their license comes up I think something can be done about
that as well. Now then, in the meantime, Selby, if you
could arrange to prosecute the proprietor for some of his

past gambling, I think it would be an excellent lesson."

Selby said, "I've been considering the matter. Of course, it takes evidence to prosecute. However, I have enough evidence which I picked up this morning to justify me in prosecuting."

"May I ask what it is?" Stapleton asked.

Selby took from his vest pocket the folded I O U which George Stapleton had given. "The sheriff and I found a game running there this morning," he said. "Triggs, the proprietor, endeavored to explain that the parties were merely playing for chips and that no money was involved, but I heard your son make a bet and his I O U for one hundred dollars, over his signature, was in the pot. Now . . ."

Stapleton frowned. "Pardon me if I interrupt, Selby, because I think I understand the circumstances, and I think I know what you're going to say. Now, Selby, I'm very anxious to see that the Palm Thatch is closed up. I feel that it will be much better for this community if the place is put out of business, but I don't wish to have the name of Stapleton involved in any way. Therefore, I feel it will be much better for you to overlook anything you found there this morning and prosecute on some other gambling game."

Selby folded the I O U and put it back in his vest pocket. "I have no evidence of any other game," he said.

Stapleton frowned. "It's rather embarrassing, but you're a man of discretion, Selby, and, I may add, a man of ability. You undoubtedly will know how to handle it. All that I wanted to suggest to you was that you keep the name of my son entirely out of it."

Selby said, "I haven't determined whether I'm going to prosecute on this morning's game or not."

"But I've just explained to you," Stapleton said, impatiently, "that I can't afford to have the name of Stapleton connected with a criminal proceeding in this county. I can't afford to have my son mixed up in a road house gambling mess."

Selby went on evenly, "If I do decide to prosecute, of

course I'll have to use this I O U in evidence. In case I shouldn't prosecute, you may rest assured that my office will give the matter no publicity."

Stapleton's face flushed a brick-red. "I'm wondering," he said, "if you entirely understood me, Mr. Selby. I don't want you to prosecute any gambling charge which will involve my son."

"So I understood," Selby said.

Stapleton settled back in his chair, and smiled. "That's all right, then. I was afraid you hadn't understood me."

Selby got to his feet and said, "I understood you perfectly, Mr. Stapleton." Stapleton picked up a half-smoked cigar, puffed complacently and nodded. "I think," Selby went on, "that the misunderstanding was entirely on your side. I don't think *you* understood *me*."

"What do you mean?" Stapleton asked.

"I mean," Selby said, "that I don't think you understood me when I told you I might decide to prosecute Triggs on account of what I saw there this morning."

Stapleton got to his feet. "Are you ignoring my request to keep my son's name out of this?"

"I'm not ignoring your request," Selby said. "I'm faced with a problem. If I decide my duty compels me to prosecute, I shall prosecute."

"Under those circumstances," Stapleton said, "I'm going to ask you to return to me the I O U which you have there."

"I'm sorry," Selby said, "that is evidence."

"You mean you'll use that in evidence against my son?"

"Not against your son, against Oscar Triggs."

"It amounts to the same thing." Selby shrugged his shoulders. Stapleton clenched his fists, placed them before him on the desk, stood leaning forward, his arms stiff, his weight on his clenched fists. "Selby," he said, "if I understand you correctly, you're making a major political mistake."

Selby smiled and said, "I think you understand me, then, Mr. Stapleton."

Stapleton glowered at him. "Look here, Selby. I'm too busy to mix much in local politics. Now are you seeking

to embarrass me because I failed to come to
your support during the last campaign?"

"Not a bit," Selby assured him.

"There are going to be other campaigns coming, you
know," Stapleton warned, "and I can always take time
from my business when my own interests demand."

"I know that."

"You'll want to be re-elected."

"Perhaps."

"I think you appreciate that my influence in the community is not trivial."

"I do," Selby told him, "but I want you to understand
this, Mr. Stapleton: I was elected to a term of office to
do my duty as I saw fit. I'm going to do it regardless of
whom it involves."

Stapleton, his face twitching, his voice edged with an-
ger, said, "You're making this exceedingly difficult for
me, Selby."

"I'm sorry," Selby remarked in a voice which showed
no contrition.

"There was one other matter I had to take up," Stapleton said, "a matter so personal, so completely and entirely removed from anything I had considered within
the realm of possibility, that I could hardly believe my
ears when Inez communicated the facts to me."

"You mean about the whiskey?" Selby asked.

"I mean about the whiskey. Will you kindly explain to
me just why you are endeavoring to use the power of
your office—in fact I might even say misuse the power of
your office—to inquire into a private purchase of whiskey
which my daughter made?"

Selby said, "I was trying to find out where a certain
bottle of whiskey had been purchased, and by whom it
had been purchased. In the course of my inquiries I
found that your daughter had purchased a dozen bottles
for you as a birthday present."

"And do you contend that that purchase was in anywise illegal?"   •

"Certainly not."

"I fail to see, then, how your office can be interested in it."

"My office is interested in it," Selby said, "because it is collecting evidence."

"Evidence of what?"

"Evidence of an attempted crime."

"I think your office will do a lot better if it confines its activities to crimes which have been committed and not annoy private citizens by inquiring into their private affairs because of crimes which *might* have been committed."

"Possibly," Selby said affably. "You have your ideas about how your business should be run; I have my ideas about how my office should be run."

Color surged into Stapleton's face, remained congested just beneath the skin, but his voice managed to maintain its steadiness. "I'm afraid, Selby," he said, with a savage attempt at being patronizing, "you have completely lost your sense of perspective. I'm afraid being elected to an underpaid office in a relatively unimportant county has given you exaggerated ideas of your own authority and importance."

"All right," Selby told him. "Having dispensed with those preliminaries, we'll now take up the question of the whiskey. What became of those dozen bottles of whiskey your daughter gave you?"

"Am I to understand," Stapleton asked, "that your office considers it possible that *I* took a bottle of whiskey down to a cabin and gave it to an impecunious hitch-hiker, a traveling vagabond, whose sole claim to distinction is that he was contemplating murder, whose immediate family consists of a daughter of such lax morality that she cheerfully acknowledges the birth of an illegitimate child?"

"You're to understand," Selby said, standing with his feet planted apart, his jaw pushed forward, "that I want to know what became of the twelve bottles of whiskey your daughter gave you."

"As it happens," Stapleton said, "I have accounted for each of those bottles. I took two of them with me in my baggage. There are four left at the house. The other six have been consumed, by myself and my friends."

"You're positive of that?"

"Absolutely."

"When you went back East on this last trip there were only six bottles left?"

"That's right."

Selby said, "I don't want to seem insistent, Mr. Stapleton, but I consider that it's of prime importance that I trace that bottle of whiskey. Circumstances would rather seem to indicate that it came from your supply."

"I don't care what the circumstances indicate," Stapleton said, "it's impossible."

"And George didn't take a bottle from your case?"

"Preposterous!" Stapleton said. "George has money enough to buy his own whiskey."

"Those six bottles which were consumed were consumed some time ago?" Selby asked.

"My birthday was some six weeks ago. I went East about a month ago. As I remember it, four bottles were consumed during the night of my birthday celebration. I took out two bottles from the balance and kept them in my study. I personally remember emptying both of those bottles. . . . Perhaps you wouldn't mind telling me, Mr. Selby, exactly why it is you're so anxious to pin this bottle of whiskey on George."

"I'm not anxious to pin anything on George," Selby said. "I'm anxious to trace the bottle of whiskey. I want to find out who was in that cabin with Watkins before he died. When I find that out, I'll be that much nearer finding out whom Watkins intended to kill."

"And when you have found *that* out," Stapleton asked, with ponderous sarcasm, "exactly how far will the welfare of this county have been advanced?"

"I don't know. I'm not a psychic. I'm a public officer. The case will at least have been cleared up and closed. My duty will have been done."

"I would say," Stapleton said, "that the case was closed when the intended murderer met an accidental death, a death which would seem to indicate a certain rather poetic justice."

"I'll consider it closed," Selby said, "when all of the

facts dovetail. Until they do, I'm going to continue my investigations."

"You may or may not be interested to learn," Stapleton remarked icily, "that on my trips, I have from time to time been in contact with some of the police commissioners and some of the officials in the Department of Justice, as well as with the more important law enforcement officers in the larger centers of population. To be perfectly frank with you, Selby, you men in these outlying rural communities, who are elected to office not because of any particular qualifications which fit you for the detection of crime, but merely because of a political expediency, can't hold a candle with these crime specialists. These men consider a case closed whenever any danger to the community is past.

"You have made this interview unnecessarily embarrassing to me personally. I think that the authority which the taxpayers have *temporarily* vested in you has gone to your head. But, if you want to overlook matters, listen to reason and consider this upon an amicable basis, my last bit of advice to you would be to follow in the footsteps of these abler and wiser men, men who are rich in experience, well grounded in the fundamentals of their profession, men with a far more mature outlook. In short, I would suggest you drop this entire matter immediately, —in which event we will forget what has passed between us here in the office."

Selby said doggedly, "I'm sorry, Mr. Stapleton, but I'm running my office. I have my own peculiar theories about the detection of crime. I believe that when we have a true explanation of any human activity all the facts are going to dovetail. Until they do, I never consider a case solved."

"Yes," Stapleton said, "your theories of crime are, as you yourself have so aptly characterized them—peculiar."

Selby said, "Well, I think that about covers things," turned and started toward the door to the outer office. With his hand on the knob, he stopped and swung back to face Stapleton. "If," he said, "you're trying to cover up anything about one of those bottles of whiskey, I'm

giving you a last opportunity to say so. Otherwise, someone's apt to get hurt."

Stapleton gripped the edge of the desk. "Damn your
impertinence, Selby," he said. "I have never been so in-
sulted, particularly in this community, a community
which I have helped to build, a community in which my
enterprises are a very large economic factor. . . . Selby,
I hate to part with you under these conditions. I think
you realize that my daughter regards you as a very close
and valued friend. She holds you in the highest regard.
For her sake, I wish you would reconsider your decision,
and I deem it my duty to warn you that if you don't, I
am going to throw every bit of influence which I command in this community against allowing you to continue in office."

Selby opened the door, paused on the threshold to say,
"That's your privilege. Play politics as much as you like.
But don't try to cover up any evidence, Mr. Stapleton.
You may feel we don't hold a candle to the officers you
meet in the big cities, but I might surprise you. I might
even turn up holding a candle!" And with that, Selby
banged the door behind him and crossed the outer office,
conscious of the startled faces of those in the waiting
room who had heard his parting thrust at Stapleton.

By the time Selby had driven back to the center of
town, *The Blade* was on the street. Selby picked up a
copy from a newsboy, drove to his apartment house, and
sat in his apartment, reading. As Sylvia had predicted,
the paper, after reporting the finding of the body, paid
editorial attention to Selby's refusal to divulge the names
of the witnesses.

"It is to be regretted that the district attorney of this
county is so young and impressionable. His refusal to disclose the names of persons who occupied the cabin in
which the dead man was found, is, in our opinion, a major blunder. By the time the smoke clears away, it will
probably turn out that Emil Watkins was merely a hitch-
hiker who sought an opportunity to separate the occupants of the cabin from some of their worldly wealth at
the point of a gun. However, he was cold and, while wait-

ing for his prospective victims to return, lit the gas heater, with fatal consequences. Even so, the taxpayers of this community are entitled to the fullest investigation of the entire affair. In the event the dead man entered the cabin with some other sinister purpose in mind, it is only fair that the taxpayers should know about it. It is only right that the authorities should know about it. The secret, if there is such a secret, doubtless lies locked in the minds of these two young men, who *claim* to have been occupying one cabin while their feminine companions occupied another.

"Gallantry is all right in its place, but that place is not in a public office. It is bad enough to have attractive women using their sex appeal on juries and securing verdicts of acquittal in cases of willful homicide, without having them use their wiles on a young, impressionable, and relatively inexperienced district attorney, who so completely loses his head that he speeds material witnesses out of the county and clothes their identities in an aura of mystery.

"The people of this city are entitled to the facts. Douglas Selby is no oracle to determine what they shall know and what they shall not know. Otto Larkin, the able, successful, and above all, experienced chief of police of Madison City, is powerless to act because the affair took place entirely without the city limits. However, Larkin admitted to a *Blade* reporter that had the crime been within the city limits those two young women would never have been permitted to leave until their story had been checked and rechecked, until their lives had been subjected to the most rigid scrutiny.

"Be that as it may, it is the function of *The Blade* to gather news and to report that news to its subscribers. Despite the fact that the public officials of this county seem to have entered into a conspiracy to keep facts from their constituents, *The Blade* promises to make unrelenting effort to find and interview these two young women. The general public will then have an opportunity to pass upon their credibility and the probability of their stories.

"There is much local furor about a national dictatorship, but how about it when a young, inexperienced, impressionable, headstrong and opinionated county official sets himself up as a court of last resort to censor what news shall be passed on to the people and what shall be completely suppressed by the simple expedient of denying the names of material witnesses to the news-gathering bodies?

"This merely emphasizes what we pointed out to the voters during the last campaign, to wit, that maturity, experience, and a general knowledge of the world are as much a part of the qualifications of an efficient prosecutor as a knowledge of the law. It is to be hoped that before the next election takes place, Douglas Selby will have learned the fallacy of high-handed methods in dealing with the highly intelligent class of voters who are his constituents, and for Selby's sake, it is also to be hoped that the voters will be inclined to forgive the very flagrant blunders which he is committing with such bewildering rapidity. For his sake, let us hope the citizens of this community will overlook the high-handed manner in which, now that their votes have placed him in office, he has relegated their interests to the background of his consciousness."

Selby had just finished reading the editorial when the telephone rang and he heard Sylvia Martin's voice on the wire. "Everything okay, Doug?" she asked.

"All ready to go," he told her.

"Did you have a talk with Stapleton?"

"Yes."

"What did he say?"

"Plenty!" Selby said.

"What happened?"

"Nothing much. His blood pressure climbed up to about two hundred and forty. When I went in, he took pains to explain to me that he'd never interested himself much in local politics—you know, they're beneath the consideration of a man of such a wide sphere of influence. . . . Well, I changed all that. He's going to be interested in local politics from now on."

113

"I'm sorry, Doug," she said, "and yet, I'm glad too. It's time someone punctured him enough to let out a little of the conceit. Honestly, when I saw him at the train today I almost burst out laughing right in his face."

"Well, the fat's in the fire now," he said.

"Have you seen *The Blade?*" she asked.

"Yes, I just finished reading it."

"Just as I told you," she said. "They've got the addresses of those girls from Larkin. This is simply a build-up. They're protecting their source of information and at the same time taking a rap at you. By the time they have public curiosity sufficiently whetted, they'll try to pin something on the girls so that it will emphasize the mistake you made in letting them go. . . . Where do I meet you, Doug?"

"You have your car?"

"Yes."

"How about driving around to my apartment? I'll be in my car down in front. You can put your bus in my garage."

"Okay," she said, "I'll be there in three minutes."

Selby picked up his bag, locked his apartment, and buttoned his overcoat tightly about him against the chill of the raw west wind. A winter dusk was deepening into early darkness. Sylvia drove up in her car a minute or two after Doug had left the apartment house. He met her at the curb and said, "Drive your car into my garage, Sylvia. I've left the door open."

"Thanks, Doug. Here we go. If the garage can stand it, the car can."

She swung her car in a sharp turn, shot it into the garage, shut off the ignition, slid out from behind the wheel and said, "It rattles around in here like one piece of corn in a corn popper. What's first on the program?"

"We go down to the Palm Thatch and see what we can find out about this hostess."

"What do you want me to do, Doug?"

"I'm going to have Triggs let us into her room," Selby said. "I want you to go over her things and then tell me

114

whether you think her disappearance was carefully planned, or if she left on the spur of the moment."

"Then what do we do, Doug?"

"Then we try to find out everything we can about the dead man."

She climbed in the car beside him. He started the motor.

"Okay," she told him, "let's go. Tell me, Doug, what about your interview with Stapleton."

Selby grinned ruefully and said, "Oh, it was a swell interview. He got red in the face and told me I'd ruined my political future. I walked out of the office and paused in the doorway for a parting shot."

"What was the parting shot, Doug?"

"He told me that the local officers couldn't hold a candle to the big city detectives with whom he comes in contact, and I told him that I was going out and try to hold a candle."

"Were there people in the outer office who could hear what you said?"

Selby nodded and said, "You should have seen their eyes pop out."

"Somehow, Doug," she said thoughtfully, "I don't think it's a bad political move. You know, there are a lot of people who are just good and fed up with Stapleton's importance and the whole town toadying to him. In some ways, the town is dependent on the sugar factory, but in other ways, the sugar factory is dependent on the town. Stapleton acts as though he's the monarch of all he surveys. If you stood up and talked back to him, it'll go around town like wildfire. It may benefit you more than enough to offset anything Stapleton can do."

Selby said, "I'm glad I did it, but I wish I hadn't done it just the way I did. I did intend to ask him about that whiskey. I intended to talk with him about George. But he started right out being so patronizing and so completely filled with self-assurance that I got mad. He seemed to feel that it was only necessary for him to hand out a little soft soap, place a fatherly hand on my shoulder and tell me just what to do, and I'd fall all over myself doing it. I blew up. Hang it all, Sylvia, *I* know that I can't compete with the experienced sleuths of the big cities, but on the other hand I have *some* brains. I know that you can't have an explanation of any form of human activity unless that explanation accounts for *all* of the facts. What's more, Sylvia, I can't get over feeling that the death of this hitch-hiker is only a surface indication of a serious potential crime which remains in the background, undiscovered and completely unsuspected. So far, the various bits of evidence don't tie into any consistent explanation."

"Well," she said, "here's the Palm Thatch. We'll see what we can find out there."

Selby swung his car into the graveled parking space. They climbed the steps and rang the bell. Triggs answered the door and surveyed them anxiously. "Any news?" he asked. "Have you heard anything from Madge?"

Selby shook his head and disappointment showed in Triggs' face. "Have *you* heard anything?" Selby asked.

Triggs silently shook his head.

"We want to look in her room," Selby said.

"Why?" Triggs asked.

"I think, by checking up on her clothes and toilet articles and things of that sort, we may be able to tell something about what she had in mind when she went away."

"I've already looked," Triggs said. "She climbed out on the roof in whatever clothes she had on at the time. She didn't carry a thing with her."

"Well," Selby said, "suppose we see what we can find. Miss Martin will help. A woman can frequently see things a man would overlook." Without a word, Triggs turned and led the way up the stairs. He paused before a locked door and inserted a key. "You say this door was locked from the inside?" Selby asked.

"Yes."

"How'd you get it open?"

"Took the small blade of my pocket knife and used the point to twist the key around in the lock. Then I

pushed it out, inserted the passkey and opened
the door. I've left things just the way they were when
I came in."

Triggs unlocked the door and opened it. The room
was large and airy. At one time, when the house had been
the residence of a prosperous rancher, there had been
four large bedrooms with connecting baths. These rooms
had been but little changed when the place had been remodeled into a road house. The room reflected Madge
Trent's personality. There were nearly two dozen auto-
graphed publicity pictures of various night club perform-
ers on the walls. Toilet articles were on the dresser,
clothes in the clothes closet. The bed had been made and
then rumpled up as though someone had been lying on
top of the covers. The pillow was badly crushed. "She
flung herself down here and started to cry and laugh,"
Triggs said. Selby nodded, walked over to the bed and
examined the pillow. As though reading his mind, Triggs
said, "That was this morning."

Selby indicated the dresser, where a framed picture of
a girl, some five or six years old, smiled down at them.
"Her daughter?" Selby asked. Triggs nodded. "Where is
she now?"

"I don't know. In some girls' school somewhere.
Madge is crazy about her. She telephoned her daughter
long distance every night of the week. It didn't make
any difference what was on. She'd break away at eight
o'clock and telephone the girl."

"What's her name?" Selby asked.

"Ruby."

"Ruby Trent?"

"I don't know what last name she goes under."

Selby looked at Triggs sharply. There was a certain
latent anxiety about the man. The poised hostility was
no longer in evidence. His eyes were almost pleading.
Selby said, "I presume you're anxious to get her back."

"She's a good hostess," Triggs admitted. "She keeps
everyone in good humor."

"How many waitresses do you have?"

"Two."

117

"What time do they come on?"

"One of them comes on at seven o'clock and works until two in the morning. One comes on at eight and works until three."

"Did the waitresses talk with her much—that is, did they know a great deal about her, where her friends live or . . . ?"

"No," Triggs said. "She didn't fraternize with the waitresses at all. She thought she couldn't control them if she did."

Selby said, "All right, Triggs, we're going through her things."

Triggs stood in the doorway, watching, as Sylvia Martin made swift exploration of the bureau drawers, opened the battered half-size trunk, examined the contents of the suitcases, gave particular attention to the toilet creams. Selby opened a drawer which contained short letters scrawled in a childish hand, a few outline drawings colored with crayon. He noticed the envelopes in which these letters had been received had all apparently been destroyed. "As nearly as I can tell," Sylvia Martin announced, "she stepped out of that window just as Mr. Triggs has said, wearing whatever clothes she had on at the time. She didn't take a thing with her."

Triggs said listlessly, "That's what I told you fellows. The sheriff scared her out of her wits."

Selby faced Triggs across the bed. "That's what I wanted to talk with you about, Triggs. *Why* was she frightened?"

"Well, the idea of a sheriff coming down and accusing her of this and that . . ."

"What did he accuse her of?"

"Putting in a telephone call."

"Exactly!" Selby said. "Now, people don't get in an uncontrollable panic merely because someone asks them if they put in a telephone call. Personally, *I* think there's a lot more to this than has appeared on the surface. What's *your* guess?"

"I haven't any," Triggs said.

"Well, suppose you make one."

"What do you mean?"

Selby said, "Some time early this morning, after twelve-thirty, when the boys arrived here from the auto camp, and before two o'clock when it started to rain, someone borrowed their car and went for a ride. Do you know anything about it?"

"No."

"We have an idea," Selby said, "that it might have been Madge Trent. Would you know anything about that?"

Triggs shook his head, thought for a moment, and then said, "I don't think so. Madge was in and out, acting as hostess. She wouldn't have gone out . . ."

Sylvia, who had been rummaging around in the closet, said, "Here's something you'd better take a look at, Doug."

Selby regarded the mud-spattered black satin pumps which Sylvia handed him. "Any idea how the mud got on these, Triggs?" he asked.

Triggs studied them in silent appraisal for a second or two, then said simply, "No."

Selby went to the window, opened it and looked out. He took a flashlight from his overcoat pocket, played the beam on the shingles. The wind was abating somewhat. The fringes of the palm leaves which had been nailed on the roof, swaying back and forth in the breeze, gave forth rustling noises, a peculiar crackling rattle as though someone had been surreptitiously walking through dry grass.

Selby said, "Just a minute. I want to take a look at this." He slid over the sill and dropped to the roof. His flashlight played around on the shingles.

Triggs, standing in the window above him, said, "Notice she could walk along that roof, to the edge, and then drop down to the driveway."

"Why not drop down right here?" Selby asked.

"I don't know," Triggs said, after a moment, "but she went over to the end to drop off. I know that."

"How?"

"Because, if she'd dropped off here, tracks would have

shown in the mud, but if she'd walked along the roof to the end, she would have dropped down to the graveled driveway."

"I see," Selby said. "She didn't leave any tracks?"

"No."

Selby pocketed his flashlight, extended his hands. "All right," he said, "I'm coming up." He gripped the sill of the window, and jumped up. Triggs and Sylvia caught him under the arms. Selby dropped into the room and said, "You don't think Madge Trent took Cuttings' car and went somewhere, early this morning?"

"Frankly, Mr. Selby, I don't."

Selby persisted in his questions. "Didn't Madge Trent leave here some time around half past five this morning and go where she *could* have telephoned me at the coroner's office?"

"No, she didn't. I know that for a fact, because she and I were together. We were checking things over."

"What things?"

"Oh, various things."

"About the case?"

"Mostly about what was going to happen out here. She has this child she's supporting. Her job naturally depends on what I take in. If you'd start putting the screws down on me, it would affect my income and that would mean Madge would find herself out of a job."

"You told her that?"

"Yes, we talked it over."

"Then, naturally she was anxious that I wouldn't prosecute."

"I think so, yes . . . naturally, of course."

"And young Stapleton was anxious that I shouldn't do any prosecuting," Selby said. Triggs said nothing. "And Charles DeWitt Stapleton doesn't want me to prosecute on any case which will involve his son." Triggs' face showed his relief. "It didn't do any good," Selby remarked, watching Triggs.

"It . . . er . . . What's that?" Triggs asked.

"It didn't do any good," Selby repeated. "I don't like to have other people dictate the policies of my office."

"Oh," Triggs observed, his tone flat and without expression. "I see."

"You have a car here, Triggs?"

"Yes."

"Was it missing?"

"When?"

"At any time, either last night or today."

"No."

"Your hostess didn't borrow it when she left?"

"No."

Selby nodded, glanced across at Sylvia and said, "Well, we have work to do. We'd better get started."

Triggs said, "You'll let me know if you hear anything from Madge Trent? I'm anxious about her."

"I'll let you know," Selby said. "We're taking these shoes of hers with us for evidence." He escorted Sylvia back to the car.

As Triggs closed the front door, and Selby pressed the starter on the car, Sylvia said, "He certainly seems anxious to co-operate, Doug, but he doesn't ring true. He's keeping something from us."

Selby said, "Well, I think we can locate her. She telephoned her daughter every night. We'll trace these calls, locate the school where her daughter's staying, and see if she calls tonight. That's one way of reaching her Triggs has overlooked."

Sylvia was dubious. "Somehow, Doug, I can't picture Triggs overlooking anything."

CHAPTER XIII

MRS. AGNES LOCKHEART showed surprise that the district attorney of Madison County should pay her a personal, and apparently official, call. When she had adjusted herself to the situation and escorted her visitors into the reception room, she sat anxiously on the edge of a chair, looking from one to the other. Tall, brunette, and with high cheekbones, her intense black eyes blinked studiously from behind her spectacles.

Selby said, "I'll get right down to business, Mrs. Lockheart. Time is short. You have a child here named Ruby Trent?"

"Yes."

"How long has she been with you?"

"A little over a year."

"What does her mother do?"

She hesitated a moment and then said, "I don't know exactly. I don't think she's a secretary. She's in business somewhere. She travels around the country quite a bit and . . . and always sends in her checks promptly on the first and the fifteenth."

"Where was she when you last heard from her?"

"In Madison City."

"She calls up her child every night?"

"Yes, sir, she does."

"Any fixed time?"

"Yes, eight. The call always comes through right about that time. She doesn't vary more than a few minutes one way or another, and I think that variation is due to delays in the long distance connections."

"She uses a party-to-party call?"

"No, a station-to-station call. I'm always near the telephone with the child, ready to talk. You see, Mrs. Trent is . . . well, she had a disagreeable experience in another school. Her daughter was ill and they didn't tell Mrs. Trent anything about it. The woman in charge diagnosed it as a minor illness. It turned out it was something rather serious, and it was only due to the fact that Mrs. Trent happened to call up that she found out about it. She dashed down to the school and rushed the child to a hospital. It was an appendix and the doctors said an hour more would have resulted in a rupture."

"So she switched schools, brought the child to you, and calls up every night?" Selby asked.

"Yes."

Selby looked at his watch. "It's seven-forty-five. I'm going to ask you to do something, Mrs. Lockheart, and,

incidentally, this is an official request. We're
going to wait here. Now, when that call comes in at eight
o'clock, I want you to find out where Mrs. Trent is.
Tell her you have an important letter to write her. . . .
Or that you'd like to discuss something with her, and
suggest that you'll run out and see her if she's not too
far from here, and bring Ruby with you."

Mrs. Lockheart's face showed a complete lack of enthusiasm. "Would you mind telling me just what you
have in mind?" she asked.

Selby said, "I'm very sorry, but it's out of the question. However, circumstances make it absolutely necessary for me to have a talk with Mrs. Trent."

"I suppose I *can* do it," Mrs. Lockheart said reluctantly.

"And, so we don't unnecessarily frighten the child,
won't it be better to have her brought in where we can
get acquainted with her now?"

Mrs. Lockheart nodded. She pressed a button, and
when the door was opened by a plump, cheerful young
woman, said, "Please bring Ruby Trent here at once.
We'll take the telephone call from her mother here."

The young woman flashed a curious glance at Selby
and Sylvia Martin, then noiselessly retired. A few moments later, she returned with a golden-haired girl. Selby,
giving one look at her twinkling eyes, at the upturned
nose and the rosebud mouth, recognized the girl whose
photograph he had seen in the hostess' room at the Palm
Thatch. "Hello, young lady," Selby said, stretching out
his hands.

She held back. Sylvia said, "I live up in Madison City
where your mother is. Do you know where that is?"

The girl pointed an indefinite finger and said, "It's up
there. Do you know my mamma?"

"Yes, indeed," Sylvia said.

"Come on," Selby invited.

She studied him with wide blue eyes for a moment,
then came across to him. "That's better," Selby told her,
seating her on his knee. "What do you and your mother
talk about when she telephones?"

The child's eyes lit with enthusiasm. "There's a mamma rabbit and a wicked coyote. My mamma tells me a little bit every night."

Mrs. Lockheart said, "She's really an exceedingly unusual child, never gives us one bit of trouble, and she has a remarkable artistic sense. I hope she has an opportunity to develop in her art work."

"What was the last your mother told you about the rabbit?" Sylvia asked.

"That was last night. The rabbit had gone out in the woods to get some nice green things to eat. She was bringing them home in a basket when the wicked coyote jumped out and chased her. The rabbit ran and ran, just as hard as she could. She could feel the coyote's breath blowing her fur. It was a hot breath and smelled like coyotes' breaths do." Her eyes were big and excited. "It was still a lo-o-o-ng ways to home, and just two more jumps and the wicked coyote would have grabbed the nice mamma rabbit. Then, all of a sudden, the mamma rabbit saw a hole in the bank and jumped into that hole and the coyote couldn't get in."

"Then what happened?"

"Then the coyote began to dig and dig and dig, and tried to dig the hole out. And the mamma rabbit squeezed back just as far as she could, but she couldn't get back very far, and the coyote's paws were just making the dirt fly."

"And then?" Sylvia asked.

"That's as far as we got last night," the girl said. "Mamma is going to tell me some more tonight."

"How long has your mother been telling you about the rabbit's adventures?" Sylvia asked.

"Oh, for a long, long time."

Mrs. Lockheart laughed and said, "I have her tell *me* the adventures just as soon as her mother finishes. It's a wonderful training for the child. She's learned to lose all self-consciousness and to make her recitals very dramatic."

"So I've noticed," Sylvia said. "I'm on pins and needles to find what's going to happen next."

Ruby regarded her in solemn appraisal.

"The rabbit's father was killed when she was just a little tiny bit of a rabbit, and the mamma rabbit had to grow up all by herself. And then she got married and had little baby rabbits and their papa ran away and left her with all the babies, and now she has to go out and work so she can bring home things to eat."

"How many babies?" Sylvia asked.

"Two. Edith Rabbit and Oscar Rabbit. They're very nice. Oscar is selfish. Oscar always wants to get the best of everything. When the mamma rabbit brings things home, why Edith Rabbit helps Mother with the basket. But Oscar Rabbit jumps right into the food and starts to eat. He's an awfully fat rabbit. Edith isn't fat."

Selby looked at his watch. "Well, it's almost eight o'clock. It won't be long now until we hear what happened to the wicked coyote."

They waited for several minutes, and felt the strain of waiting, listening for the phone to ring. Occasionally they exchanged short comments, mostly brief questions which were answered with monosyllables. As Selby looked at his watch for the fourth time, Mrs. Lockheart said, "Sometimes she's fifteen or twenty minutes late. It takes a while to get the connection through, but she always puts in the call right at eight o'clock and I always keep Ruby up until after her mother has called. Then Ruby goes to bed to think about the rabbit."

"How many children have you here?" Selby asked.

"We have seventeen now."

"I suppose you have rather complete records of their names, places of birth, parents, and all of that."

"Quite complete, yes."

"I wonder if you'd mind letting me see the record on this young lady."

Mrs. Lockheart said, "You'll have to excuse me just a moment. The records are in my office." She left the room and Ruby said to Selby, "You don't suppose the coyote dug in and got the mamma rabbit, do you?"

"Well," Selby said gravely, "coyotes are very fierce and wicked, but somehow I think Mamma Rabbit will be all right. What kind of a hole did she run into? Was it a hole made by some other animal or just a place under a rock?"

"It was a hole that had been dug out by something, but it got small after it went in a ways," Ruby said, with wide-eyed seriousness. "The mamma rabbit thought when she ran into the hole it would be a good place to run way in and hide, but after she got in a little ways, she found that she couldn't go any farther, and then the wicked coyote started to dig away the dirt."

"Well, you'll probably know in a few minutes just what happened," Selby said. "I suppose that . . ." He broke off as Mrs. Lockheart came back and handed him the card. Selby studied it for a moment, then said, "I see there's a blank here for the names of the grandparents. This blank hasn't been filled in. Does this mean the child's grandparents are dead?"

"Not necessarily," Mrs. Lockheart said. "Sometimes we don't go to the trouble of writing in all that information. It depends on the circumstances. If there's a possibility the child might be abandoned in our care, we want to know all about the details of its family. Otherwise, we don't care for so much statistical information."

"Born in Malden, Massachusetts," Selby read from the card. "That's a long ways from here, Ruby."

"A long, long way," she told him. "You have to ride for days and days on a train to get here from Malden."

Sylvia looked at her wrist watch. Mrs. Lockheart said, "Tell me, Mr. Selby, your interest in the matter doesn't indicate that this regular telephone call may be postponed, does it?"

"I don't know," Selby admitted. "I'm hoping it won't."

There followed another awkward interval of waiting. Ruby Trent, sitting in Selby's lap, slid over so that her head lay on his shoulder. She yawned, rubbed her eyes and smiled. "I want to know about the coyote," she said drowsily.

"How would you like to lie down until your mother calls, and then come and talk with her?" Mrs. Lockheart asked sympathetically.

Ruby shook her head vigorously. "No, I want to wait right here."

Selby started rocking her. "Perhaps," he said, glancing over the child's shoulder at Sylvia Martin, "it would be a good plan for me to go out and hunt the coyote. Perhaps I should chase him away from the hole where the mamma rabbit is hiding."

The child pushed sleep from her eyes to stare up at him. "Could you do that?" she asked.

"I think so," Selby said. "At any rate, I think perhaps I'd better go and try. But if I do that, you'll have to promise to go to bed and wait. Perhaps that's why your mother isn't telephoning. She hasn't found out yet just what's going to happen. The coyote has the mamma rabbit trapped in the hole and the mamma rabbit can't get out, and your mother's hoping someone will come and chase the coyote away."

The child, abruptly reaching a wordless decision, slid to the floor, walked across the room to Mrs. Lockheart and said, "All right."

Mrs. Lockheart scooped her up in her arms. "I'll take you upstairs."

Selby got to his feet. "I think we'll start hunting the coyote," he said. "If the call should come in in my absence, will you please explain that it's quite important that I have an interview at once?"

"I will," she said. "Where can I reach you?"

"You can leave any message by calling Sheriff Brandon's office at Madison City," Selby said. "Good night, Ruby."

"Good night," she said gravely. "You go chase that coyote."

CHAPTER XIV

OUTSIDE in the car, Sylvia Martin said, "Doug, listening to that story of the mamma rabbit, I had a most peculiar feeling. I felt that the adventures Madge Trent had been telling her daughter as a continued bedtime story were real, particularly that part about the mamma rabbit being chased by the wicked coyote."

Selby nodded gravely. "I felt the same way. Obviously, however, the thing is impossible. She told the little girl this last episode at eight o'clock last night. At that time there had been no hitch-hiker in her life, no possible intimation of his death, no telephone call, telling me it was a murder, no visit by the sheriff, no accusation that she had placed that call. . . ."

"I'm not so certain, Doug," she interrupted. "How about the 'Oscar Rabbit' who grabbed everything from the basket? I feel certain she meant Oscar Triggs. I'll bet this story is a paraphrase of Madge Trent's own adventures."

"You *may* be right," Selby conceded.

"And," she went on, "I naturally wondered the same thing you did about the child's grandparents." Selby raised his eyebrows. "Oh, don't try to hold out on me, Doug Selby," she said. "I know what you have in mind. You thought that perhaps Ruby Trent is the granddaughter that was mentioned in the letters we found on the dead man."

"Well, if that's the case," Selby said, "Madge Trent must be the missing daughter, Marcia."

"Doug, I feel that it's right, I feel that it must be right. . . . Madge Trent never saw the man's body, did she?"

"No," Selby said, "she didn't. Of course, at the time, I had no intimation that there was any possible connection between the dead man and the people of the Palm Thatch—other than through the two boys."

"Doug," she said, "I want to telephone this story in to the paper. Is there any reason why I can't say that your office is working on the theory that the missing night club hostess may have been the daughter of the man who was murdered?"

"Better just hint at the possibility," Selby told her. "However, I think the more publicity this thing has, the better."

"Gosh, Doug, what a whale of a story this is going to

make—a little girl waiting for her mother to
tell her whether the mamma rabbit got away from the
wicked coyote, and the telephone not ringing."

Selby said, "I'm going to stop and call the sheriff's office in Madison City, Sylvia. You can put in a call for
your paper at the same time. We passed a large hotel
about a mile back. It'll have telephone booths."

Selby drove to the hotel. While Sylvia Martin was calling her paper, he talked with the under-sheriff who was
on night duty in the courthouse. "We've got some dope
on an Emil Watkins, who was a carpenter," the under-
sheriff said. "He's supposed to have left some things with
a Bob Praile who's connected with the Carpenters' Union
down in San Diego. We got Praile on the telephone and
he says that he's holding some things Watkins left in
storage, a tool chest and a couple of trunks. He said Watkins had some mail forwarded to him there at San
Diego; that he was a peculiar chap, narrow-minded,
opinionated, but honest and fair. You could never convince him of anything in an argument. Now then, a couple of months ago, Watkins left these trunks and Praile
hasn't seen him since."

"That's fine," Selby said. "I'll call Praile right away."

"You won't need to," the deputy said. "I told him that
you were in Oceanside and would come right down to
San Diego to hunt him up; that you'd want to see what
was in the trunks. I gave him a description of this man,
Watkins, we found up here and the description checks
all right, so I guess we've got the right man."

"That's fine," Selby said. "How about Rex? Did he go
to San Francisco all right?"

"No, he didn't," the deputy said. "Something came up
and he decided he'd wait and go on the plane tomorrow."

Selby frowned. "I wanted him to go up on the train
tonight."

"Well, he can take an early plane and get there at just
the same time," the deputy said. "And something came
up here he wanted to investigate. He's out somewhere
now. I'll tell him you called."

"All right," Selby said. "And here's another thing: a

Mrs. Lockheart may call up and give you Madge Trent's address. If she does, get in touch with the Los Angeles sheriff's office and have her picked up immediately. I'm on my way to San Diego."

CHAPTER XV

THE RAW west wind had gone down. Stars shone unwinkingly from a cloudless sky. But the gale had kicked up a sea which came crashing in on the graveled beaches, bursting into spray on the promontories. A moon but little past the full climbed up over the mountains to the left as Selby's car sped along the highway which at times followed the mesa land, at times dipped down, to run along the shores of the pounding ocean. Sylvia Martin cuddled up close to Selby. "Doug," she said, "did it ever impress you as being queer how much more you can find out about people after they're dead than while they're alive?"

"What do you mean?" he asked.

"People always keep fences up while they're alive. You never get to know them. Take this hitch-hiker, for instance. You and the sheriff stopped him and talked with him. You didn't find out anything. He was just an ordinary hitch-hiker. Now we start prying into his past, and digging up little things, and he commences to become a character. We learn things he would never have admitted while he was alive. Look at what we've discovered from the letters we found in his pocket.

"There's a man who was a stern, righteous father. His daughter loved him in her way, and he loved her in his; but she put herself out of his life. She had a daughter. This carpenter, with his stern ideas, was a grandfather, but had never seen his grandchild. His conventional ideas of morality are probably the safest, yet they caused him to deny himself the love of his daughter. He denied himself a chance to know his granddaughter simply because he regarded as a sin something his daughter regarded as natural and moral. She loved this young man who couldn't or wouldn't marry her. She thought they were going to be married some time in the future. . . . I wonder if her ideas changed. . . . Perhaps she realized how much wisdom was back of the conventions. . . . And how much suffering there was for Watkins. . . . Somehow, Doug, it's such a simple thing and yet so real. It gets in your mind and just sticks."

Selby nodded, drove the car in musing silence for a while. Sylvia, her head pillowed on his shoulder, dropped off to sleep. The moon moved higher in the heavens, illuminating the tossing waters of the restless ocean, silvering the spray kicked up by the booming breakers against the headlands. Foam from the water which dashed, hissing, up the slopes of rounded water-worn pebbles showed in the moonlight as a line dividing land and water. Selby, for the moment, forgot the grim nature of his mission, gave himself up to the beauty of the night, the sense of companionship with the young woman curled up so naturally at his side.

They sped swiftly through the streets of San Diego, found Bob Praile waiting for them at the address he had given. He examined Selby's credentials, identified the picture of the dead hitch-hiker which Selby showed him, and said, "Okay, Mr. Selby, it's all yours, so far as I'm concerned. Go ahead and open up the baggage if you want to."

"I don't want to take anything," Selby said, "I just want to look through these things, and I think you'd better be with me in order to check what I find."

"All right," Praile said, "go to it."

They opened the trunks. Sylvia, standing slightly to one side, scribbled notes on copy paper with a soft pencil, her fingers making the pencil fairly fly over the paper.

Everything about the trunks was indicative of the character of the man who had packed them. The clothes were neatly arranged and folded. The overalls were scrupulously clean. Holes had been carefully darned. In one of the trunks, Selby found an old photograph showing Emil Watkins and his bride. The picture had evidently been taken some thirty years earlier, but even then the grim, uncompromising lines had made themselves manifest about the man's mouth. The package of envelopes tied together with a string disclosed various unimportant letters. Among them was a receipted bill from a San Diego hospital.

"Any idea what this bill is?" Selby asked Praile.

"None whatever. I didn't know anything about him. He came in here and got mail, and when he left he wanted to leave this stuff here for a few weeks."

"He didn't say where he was going?"

"No."

Selby said, "This bill is dated a month ago. I think I'll take it along, if you don't mind. I'll either bring it back to you or mail it back and you can put it with the other things."

"Okay by me," Praile said. "Since he's dead, what are we supposed to do with the stuff?"

"The administrator of his estate will get in touch with you," Selby said. "He has a daughter somewhere. Just keep the stuff until we can get her located."

"All right by me," Praile said cheerfully, his eyes appraising Sylvia Martin's trim figure with evident approval. "Anything else I can help you with?"

"Nothing," Selby said. "Thanks."

They drove to the hospital. Selby showed the bill to the young woman at the desk. She looked up various records, then nodded and said, "The patient's name was Marcia Watkins. She died. He paid the bill."

"Dead!" Sylvia Martin exclaimed incredulously.

The nurse nodded.

"I wonder," Selby said, "if you could give me the name of someone who knows something about the case— that is, some of the nurses who were on duty and . . ."

"She had a special, I believe. Let me see. . . . Yes, two specials. One of them happens to be on duty here in the hospital. Would you like to talk with her?"

"Very much," Selby said.

The young woman picked up a telephone and said, "Get me the fourth floor. . . . Hello, Miss Quincy

. . . ? What's Madeline Dixon doing . . . ?
Do you suppose she could come to the phone for a min-
ute . . . ? Hello, Miss Dixon, this is the office. A Mr.
Selby, district attorney from Madison County, is here,
trying to get some information about Marcia Watkins.
You were on that case as a special about a month ago. . . .
Yes, that's the one. . . . All right, if you can. Thanks."

She dropped the receiver back into place and said,
"Miss Dixon will be here in just a moment. Just be
seated, please."

Selby walked to the window, stood staring out at the
cold radiance of the moonlit night. Sylvia came to stand
at his side. "Dead!" Sylvia said. "That's the last thing I
expected. I'd have sworn Marcia Watkins and Madge
Trent were the same. But if Marcia Watkins is dead,
that's an end to *that* theory."

Selby nodded. "She evidently sent for him when she
became ill. . . . She probably came here to see him;
perhaps she was suffering from some incurable trouble
. . . he must have forgiven her. He had her in a private
room, with two special nurses. It looks as though . . ."

He turned from the window as a trimly uniformed
nurse, with black hair and alert black eyes, entered the
room. "Mr. Selby?" she asked.

"Yes."

"I'm Miss Dixon."

"Sit down, Miss Dixon," Selby invited. "This is Miss
Martin from Madison City. I wanted to find out anything you could tell me about this Watkins case. First,
however, I'd like to have you look at a photograph."

Selby took from his pocket a photograph of the dead
hitch-hiker. The nurse looked at it thoughtfully and said,
"Yes, that's her father."

"Can you tell me what happened?" Selby asked.

"She was injured in an automobile accident. I think
she'd come to San Diego to find her father, and she was
hit about ten o'clock one night. She was picked up unconscious and remained unconscious, as I remember it,
until around four in the morning. . . . Of course, Mr.
Selby, I'm giving you this from recollection. I didn't

come on duty myself until nine o'clock in the morning. That was after they'd identified her and located her father."

"Go ahead," Selby said.

"Her father had her put in a private room and employed special nurses. I came on day duty and was on duty all that day. A night nurse took over, and I was on duty the next day when she died."

"What time was that?" Selby asked.

"Some time in the afternoon," she said. "I can't remember exactly when."

"Did you," Selby asked, "hear any of the conversations between the father and the daughter?"

She glanced at him sharply and said, "Just what is it you want, Mr. Selby?"

Selby said, "I'm going to put my cards on the table. The body of Emil Watkins was found in an auto camp. He died from carbon monoxide poisoning. A gas stove was going full blast."

The nurse said musingly, "I've wondered if he wouldn't commit suicide."

Selby said, "It wasn't suicide. He had a gun in his hand when we found him."

The nurse said, in the voice of one who has convinced herself, "It *must* have been suicide."

"Could you," Selby asked, "tell me something of the conversations he had with his daughter?"

"I'm afraid not, Mr. Selby," she said. "You see, those are professional confidences."

Selby was firm. "I'm afraid I'm going to have to insist on an answer. After all, the parties are dead. There's no living person to be affected."

She apparently reached a sudden decision, said, "Very well, Mr. Selby, I heard quite a bit of their conversations. The doctor didn't allow her to talk very much at first, but they said enough so I gathered what had happened. Her mother had died when she was a child. Her father had brought her up. Her father was of the old school, a stern man with a tender heart and an absolutely uncompromising moral code. The girl had gone away with a man. She expected him to marry her.

He didn't do it. There was a child and . . . well, before she died, they had it out about the child."

"What about it?" Selby asked.

"He wanted to know all about the child—where it was, and all about it. He wanted to do something for it, but . . . oh, I don't know as I can describe that scene to you so you'll really understand it. It was pathetic. I wished I could do something to help. She was lying there in the bed, dying. We all knew she was dying then. She knew it herself. Her father knew it. The father loved her, and he wanted to love his granddaughter. But to him the granddaughter was a child of sin. And Miss Watkins told him bluntly that unless he could get that idea out of his mind he was never to see the child. Evidently she'd suffered in her own childhood. She was beautiful, emotional and impulsive, just the opposite of what he was. He sat there by the bed, with his lips clamped tight, the tears streaming down his cheeks, and absolutely unforgiving. His daughter had sinned. The wages of sin were death. And what had happened was a judgment which had come to pass for what she had done. . . . And she wouldn't tell him anything about the granddaughter."

"Was the child in San Diego with her?" Selby asked.

"Apparently not. I think it was in a school somewhere. Miss Watkins was pretty close-mouthed about all of that. She didn't want to give him any clew to work on. . . . He was so stern, so self-righteous, so unforgiving, that . . . that . . . that I could have kicked him. I'd have done it, too, if it hadn't been he was so sincere, so pitifully earnest. He was torturing himself. But he was as hard as granite. It was a question of his conventional ideas against hers. . . . And so she carried her secret to the grave with her."

"Why had she come to San Diego?" Selby asked. "To get work?"

"No, apparently to have a talk with him. She'd been separated from him for years. She thought it was a mistake. She thought perhaps the years might have softened him somewhat. Apparently she'd written him a few times, but had never given him an address where he could write her. She knew how to reach him because he was a carpenter and a member of the union."

"Was she driving an automobile?" Selby asked.

"No, she was a pedestrian. She was knocked down by a hit-and-run driver about ten o'clock at night. The driver was drunk, but he got away. The police asked her questions about the car. She had a general description of it, and, as I remember it, she'd tried to get the license number, but all she'd been able to see was the first figure and the letter. She either couldn't remember anything after that or hadn't seen it, I've forgotten exactly which it was. . . . You know, I thought perhaps the father would commit suicide. He took her death awfully hard. He thought it was a judgment, and all that, but just the same you could see that he loved her and he'd missed her. . . . He *should* have loved her. She had a happy, lovable disposition. She went out with a smile. You could see she loved him, too, but she wasn't going to let her child suffer because of the stigma he'd place upon it. I'll never forget how she looked at him. Her eyes were tender, but she had just as much obstinacy as he did. She died just that way."

"How about her suitcase?" Selby asked. "Wasn't there a clew somewhere in her baggage?"

"As to that," she said, "I don't know. She didn't have any baggage when she came to the hospital. She was picked up by an ambulance, taken to the Emergency, and then brought here. At first it looked as though she was going to make it, but she was injured internally. She was conscious right up to the last. She sat there, propped up in bed, growing weaker and weaker, looking across at her father. He was holding her hand and crying like a baby, but his mouth was just as thin and hard as a razor blade. We nurses see quite a bit of life—and death. This was one of the most pathetic cases I've ever had—and it was all so horribly unnecessary. He'd have loved the little granddaughter if he could only have forgotten his rigid, iron-clad conventions and let himself go."

Selby glanced at Sylvia Martin. "Thanks very much,

Miss Dixon," he said. "I think that clarifies the situation somewhat."

"I'm glad to know the final outcome of it," she said. "I'd always wondered. If you need me, Mr. Selby, you can reach me here at the hospital."

Selby thanked her, took Sylvia Martin's arm and escorted her to the door. Outside, in the still cold of the evening, Sylvia said quaveringly, "Doug, do you suppose I'll ever make a g-g-g-good rep-p-p-porter if I keep on b-b-bawling when things get like that."

He slipped his arm around her waist, walked silently with her to the car. In the automobile, she dabbed at her eyes with a handkerchief, and said, "Perhaps it's because of the way we've gone at this thing, Doug, but I get to feel that I know those people. I feel that they're closer to me than lots of the people I meet every day. They're dead and gone now, and we're prying into their lives. . . . It's something like seeing an actress on the screen after she's dead. You see her happy and vivacious, acting the part of a play, and you have three reactions all blended together—first, the story of the play which grips you, then the charm of the actress and admiration for her, and then, deep underneath, the realization beating at the back of your mind that she's dead and gone. It opens up the mysteries of life to you, makes things seem solemn and . . . oh, I can't explain it, Doug. It isn't that you're frightened, it's different from that. It's a feeling of peace and calm, but an appreciation of the futility of so much of human emotion, particularly the petty selfishnesses. Think of what a horribly futile thing that barrier was which he put up between himself and his daughter."

Selby patted her shoulder and said, "I know, Sylvia. I understand how you feel."

"Well," she said, with a little forced laugh, "that doesn't keep us from facing the facts of our own lives, Doug Selby. You're the district attorney of Madison County. I'm a reporter for *The Clarion*. I have to make a story of this that will make the newspaper readers see it the way I see it . . . and we're going to have to find out why Madge Trent didn't ring up her daughter and tell her what happened to the mamma rabbit who was chased by the wicked coyote."

Selby nodded silent acquiescence, pressed his foot on the starter and throbbed the motor into life.

CHAPTER XVI

SYLVIA said, "I want to stop and telephone the paper, Doug. Do you mind?"

"Not a bit," he told her. "I'll drive up to one of the hotels."

He drove slowly and in silence, his forehead puckered into a frown. He found a parking space near one of the hotels, slid to the curb and said, "Go to it, Sylvia, I have something I want to think out."

Ten minutes later, when she emerged from the hotel, she found him as she had left him, slumped back of the wheel, his hands pushed down deep in his overcoat pockets.

"Well," she said. "No, don't bother, Doug, I can make it." Before he could move from behind the wheel, she had opened the door, jumped in, and closed the door after her. "Why all the abstraction? Are you feeling the same way I do, Doug, or . . . ?"

"I'm toying with an idea," Selby told her, "which seems logical. Yet it's just a nebulous idea. I don't dare to go ahead with it unless I can get some proof, and I don't know how I can get any proof."

She surveyed his profile appraisingly, then said, "All right, suppose you cut me in on the idea and I'll tell you how it sounds to an unbiased listener."

Selby took his gloved hands from his pockets, tapped with the tips of the fingers on the polished wood of the steering wheel. "So far, Sylvia, we've acted on the assumption that this hitch-hiker was trying to trace his grandchild or was looking for some person whom he intended to kill, the motivation being indicated by the letters which he was carrying around with him."

She nodded as he paused, and said, "Go on, Doug."

"It seems to me," Selby said, "that even for a man of such stern convictions, with a razor-edge mouth, and all of the dogged determination in the world, it's a little bit unusual to search for the betrayer of a daughter after so many years have passed. On the other hand, Watkins had a gun and was probably intending to use it on someone. Now then, suppose we have our motivation wrong?"

"What do you mean, Doug?"

"Simply this: suppose that after his daughter's death, Watkins started out, not to avenge her honor in the generally accepted sense of the word, but for the purpose of inflicting retributive justice upon the person who was responsible for her death."

"You mean he was looking for the hit-and-run driver?" Selby nodded. "What gives you that idea, Doug?" she asked.

"Remember," Selby said, "that the girl couldn't give a very accurate description of the car, but she did recognize the first number of the license plate and the letter. Also, she had a general idea of what the car looked like. Now then, bear in mind that the Motor Vehicle Department has certain license numbers which are assigned to certain sections of the state. Each section has a letter and a number. For instance, the Imperial Valley has 'IV,' and as we go north . . ."

"Yes, yes, Doug, I know all about that. Go on. What are you getting at?"

Selby said, "Do you remember that the evidence in this case shows that George Stapleton was driving a high-powered super-charged sports job which was worth in the neighborhood of two thousand second hand, and he suddenly sold it to Cuttings for seven hundred and fifty dollars?"

"I didn't know that," she said. "You hadn't told me."

"Well, I'm telling you now," he said. "It came out incidentally when we were making a check-up on those boys."

"And you think Stapleton . . . ?" She paused, as the

full implication of what she was about to say struck her mind. "Good heavens, Doug!" she rushed on. "It's absolutely impossible. Stapleton is wild and harumscarum. He cuts a pretty wide swath, but after all, he's the son of the town's most influential man."

Selby pushed his hands back deep in his pockets. "That's exactly it," he said. "Young Stapleton has always been able to muster enough political pull to get away with anything he wanted to try. He tears along the highway at seventy and eighty miles an hour in his supercharged sport job. He doesn't pay fines. His father has a way of fixing traffic tickets. He's accustomed to driving down to the city, getting two or three cocktails under his belt, and chasing around in his automobile."

"And you think that he might have hit this girl?"

He didn't answer her immediately. His chin rested on his chest as he stared moodily at the illuminated dials on the dashboard of the automobile. Then he slowly nodded. "It would make a lot of things fit together," he said. "The girl was knocked down. She tried to get the license number, and failed, but she got part of it. That part of it was enough to give her father a pretty good line on the place where the automobile was owned. She was probably able to give him a description of the color of the car and what it looked like. So he started out trying to find the driver and bring him to justice. He knew that the car was owned somewhere near Madison City, and he started patrolling the road, on the theory that the person owning such a sporty job would have lots of money, and, having lots of money and a nice car to drive, would be apt to keep on the road pretty much between Madison City and Los Angeles.

"What he overlooked was the fact that young Stapleton wasn't anybody's fool by a long ways. He knew that if anyone had got the full license number, officers would have been pounding on his door before he got home that night. Therefore, he reasoned that it was quite possible someone had an incomplete license number, plus a description of the car. He knew that there was a chance someone might be looking for his car, without knowing whose car it was, but knowing generally where it was located. So he decided it would be a smart move to get rid of the car, have it transferred to a different section of the state, and start driving another car himself."

"Doug, I don't believe it," she said. "It doesn't sound possible."

"I know it doesn't," he told her, "but it's commencing to make sense. Now then, suppose Watkins was patrolling the highway, hoping to find that car. The reason he didn't find it was because Cuttings had taken the car out of that section of the state. But last night Cuttings came back, and Watkins spotted him. It took him some little time to find out where Cuttings was staying, but by covering the automobile camps, he finally found out. Remember that as the car passed him on the highway yesterday night, he had an opportunity to get the complete license number. Then he searched around the auto camps until he found out where the owner of that car was staying. Now, Watkins had a one-track, single-purpose mind. He was stern and self-righteous and doubtless subscribed to the doctrine of an eye for an eye and a tooth for a tooth. By the time he located the place where Cuttings was staying, Cuttings had taken the car and gone out to the Palm Thatch. Watkins decided he was going to wait for Cuttings to come back. Therefore, he managed to get into the cabin and waited for Cuttings."

"But how did he get in, Doug?" she asked.

"That," Selby said, "is something which remains to be seen."

"How are you going to find out?" she asked.

"For one thing," Selby said, "I'm going to the police station, check the records of traffic accidents, and find out just how much the police got from Marcia Watkins before she died. If I find that she described the car that hit her as a big red car with a white stripe running around it, a long, slanting back, and if the first two figures of the license show that it came from our county, then I'm going to be pretty certain."

"Gee, Doug," she said, "this *is* big! Think of what

Stapleton would do if his son should be accused of anything like that. Doug, you just don't *dare* to make a move unless you're absolutely certain of your ground."

"I don't know," he told her, "just how I can get any definite proof. The only witness is dead."

"You're going to try the police station?"

He nodded, took his hands from his pockets, snapped on the ignition switch, pushed in the starter and threw the car into gear. "We're on our way," he said, "and if this thing pans out . . . Lord, what a blow-up there's going to be! Every bit of political and financial pressure in Madison County will be brought to bear to make me lay off Stapleton."

"Doug," she said, "how about Inez?"

"What about her?"

"What difference is it going to make with her?"

"I don't know," Selby said.

"Doug, don't you think . . . Won't it be better to let Brandon handle it from here on? After all, Doug, it was one thing to stand up to Charles DeWitt Stapleton and insist that he answer questions about evidence. It's going to be another to . . . to prosecute Inez' brother for crime."

Selby shook his head doggedly. "I'm going to see this thing through," he said. He started the car, drove for several blocks silently, then brought it to a stop near the police station, and said, "You'd better sit here in the car. I'll only be in here a few minutes." He opened the door, slid out behind the steering wheel, slammed the door shut, and pounded across the pavement, the skirts of his overcoat flapping around his long legs as he walked.

Sylvia Martin burrowed down into the warm interior of the car and waited. Selby was back within fifteen minutes. "Well?" she asked.

"It looks like it," he told her. "The police say that the girl was able to give two of the license numbers—that is, the first number, and the letter. She described the car as a big red car with a white stripe around it, a long, slanting back with an extra wheel nested in the back. . . . In other words, she's described a car which, as nearly as I

142

can remember it, checks absolutely with
young Stapleton's car—that is, the one which he sold for
a fraction of its real value to Cuttings."

"You know, Doug," she warned him, "you can't prove
a thing. All you have is surmises. The woman was struck
by a car which was registered in our section of the state, *if*
she didn't make any mistake in reading the license number.
It's a big red car with a white stripe, and that's all she could
remember. That's all she saw. And she's dead. She can't
testify. Now, I admit, if you'd known this the morning
after the accident, you might have been able to . . ."

"I know it now," Selby said grimly, "and that's going
to be enough."

"What are you going to do?"

"We're going back to Madison City and find out where
we stand."

"Doug, you don't dare to actually accuse Stapleton—
not with the evidence you have now."

"I don't know where we're going to get any more evidence," Selby said.

"And you're going to accuse George Stapleton?"

"I'd be failing to do my duty if I didn't."

"How about the hostess, Doug?"

"I don't know," Selby said. "I can't figure where she
fits into the picture."

"Well," Sylvia asked, "what's next on the program,
Doug? Are you going back to Madison City now?"

Selby pulled a pipe from his pocket, pushed tobacco
down into the bowl, and struck a match, which he held
cupped in his hands. Sylvia watched his boyish, but reso-
lute profile while the ruddy flame of the match illuminated his features. "The police here never found out very
much about Marcia Watkins," he said. "They remember
that her father asked them to make an investigation of
the hotels and see if she'd been registered. They covered
the hotels and rooming houses but couldn't find where
she'd been staying."

"You have an idea, Doug?" she asked.

"Yes. I've been wondering. Suppose she came to San
Diego on one of the bus lines. She'd naturally have left

her suitcase checked in the bus depot while she started out to meet her father."

"If she'd done that, Doug, there'd have been a claim check in her purse."

"That's right," Selby admitted. "But she must have had baggage with her. She must have left it somewhere. Let's drive down to the bus depot anyway, Sylvia, and see what we can find out. The place where she was picked up was within a couple of blocks of there."

Selby drove to the terminal and said, "Wait here, Sylvia. I'm going in and make some inquiries."

Once more she waited while the clock on the dash of the automobile metered the minutes, then Selby emerged with a triumphant smile, carrying two suitcases. "Doug!" she exclaimed. "You've found them?"

He nodded. "It was simple," he said. "She got off the stage and told the attendant in charge of the office that she was going to place a couple of telephone calls, and asked him to keep his eye on the baggage for five or ten minutes. When she didn't show up, the attendant put her baggage in storage. He remembered the occasion as soon as I mentioned it to him, but I had to call up the police and get them to authorize a delivery to me before he'd let them go." He loaded the suitcases in the back of his car, said, "Okay, Sylvia. Here we go."

"Don't you want to see what's inside of the suitcases?"

"Not now," he told her. "We'll stop after we get out of town a ways. I want to make time back to Madison City."

He drove in close to the curb on a side street near the outskirts of the city. They switched on the dome light. He and Sylvia went through the suitcases. Sylvia's deft fingers, digging down in the folded silks, said, "Here are some papers, Doug," and brought out some envelopes, a notebook and some folded papers, held together with a rubber elastic.

The first letter which Selby unfolded gave him the desired information. It was on the stationery of a law firm from Chicago and read,

DEAR MRS. WATKINS: With reference to your request that we communicate with the father of your daughter,

Edith, who is at present in the Mid-Continental Boarding School for Children, insisting that an increase be made in the contribution which he is making toward the support of the child, please be advised that we are this day in receipt of a letter from Mr. Samuel C. Roper, an attorney in Madison City, stating that the addressee of our letter has consulted him with reference to the contents thereof; that it is the attitude of his client that the money being paid at present is purely by way of compromise, and that if any attempt on your part is made to increase the amount or to adjudicate him as the parent, the paternity will be denied and the case vigorously contested. Mr. Roper states that the amount of twenty-five dollars a month which is being contributed by his client represents the absolute maximum that his client will pay, and will immediately be discontinued in the event you try to enforce any rights you claim to have in the matter. Awaiting your further instructions, we remain   Very truly yours,

Selby glanced up from the letter, to meet Sylvia Martin's startled eyes. "Gosh, Doug," she said, "where does *that* leave us?"

"Darned if I know," Selby admitted.

"You don't suppose you could trick Roper into disclosing the identity of his client?"

"No," Selby said, "but the Chicago lawyers will know."

"How about sending them a wire, Doug?"

"We only have their office address," he said. "This is Saturday night. Tomorrow's Sunday."

"Why not wait, Doug? Or, perhaps you could get the Chicago Police to locate one of the partners."

Selby shook his head doggedly. "The paternity of the child doesn't have anything to do with this case now," he said. "The main thing to be determined right now is whether George Stapleton was the one who hit that girl. If he did, I'm going to find out about it."

"But, Doug, it's such a gamble."

"I love to gamble," he told her.

"And how about this hostess, Doug? Does that change

the situation any as far as she's concerned?"

Selby said thoughtfully, "You know, young Stapleton may very well have had some woman in the car with him at the time of the accident and it's barely possible that woman was Madge Trent."

Sylvia's eyes widened. "That," she said, "would account for darned near everything."

Selby closed Marcia Watkins' suitcase, and said, "Well, let's quit thinking about it. Try and get some sleep, Sylvia."

"When are you going to let me drive?"

"I'll drive until I get tired, and then you can spell me while I rest my eyes."

She slid down into a corner of the seat, turned sideways, drew up her knees and studied his profile. "How about a bedtime story, Mr. District Attorney," she said. "Could you tell me what happened to the little mamma rabbit and the wicked coyote?"

Selby grinned his fighting grin. "Hunters are after the wicked coyote," he said. "Let's hope they find him before he digs up the mamma rabbit."

CHAPTER XVII

SELBY was just entering Madison City when he heard the low throb of a siren behind him and on his left. He swung in toward the curb, slowed, and looked up into the grinning countenance of Rex Brandon. "Do you think you're going to a fire?" Brandon called. "Don't you know we have speed limits in this town?"

Selby put on the brakes. Brandon stopped in front of him, got out of his car and came back, to stand with one foot on the runningboard. "Hello, Sylvia," he said, and then to Doug, "What is this, business or a joy ride?"

"Who wants to know?" Selby asked, a smile twitching the corners of his mouth.

"I do," the sheriff said. "If it's business I'll let you get away with speeding, but if it's a joy ride I'm going to get you both jail sentences."

Selby said, "It's joy riding."

"Come on, Doug," Brandon told him, his face growing serious, "kick through."

"I don't want to, Rex."

"Why not?"

"Because," Selby told him, "I'm committing political suicide. I'm a leper. I don't want you to get near me, because I don't want you to be contaminated."

Sheriff Brandon surveyed the pair of them with eyes which missed nothing. "What form," he asked, "does the leprosy take?"

"Getting independent with Charles DeWitt Stapleton," Selby said.

Brandon grinned. "Shucks, I'd heard all about that already. It's all over town. I was hoping someone would do that one of these days. You know, Doug, sometimes I think his hat is awfully tight. Now I know why you wanted me to rush up to San Francisco. You wanted to have me parked out of the danger zone, didn't you?"

"That," Selby told him, "is beside the point. The real point is that Charles DeWitt Stapleton can pretty nearly control the political situation in this county if he makes up his mind to do it. Most of the time he remains neutral, assuming the position that he's too big and important to mix in local politics, and expecting whoever's elected to toady to him."

"I suppose he wanted you to keep George's name out of everything, didn't he?" Selby nodded.

The sheriff studied him with quizzical eyes. "Why didn't you agree to do what he wanted, Doug? You didn't intend to prosecute on that gambling game, did you?"

"I don't know," Selby said, "whether I'm going to prosecute or not, but I do know that I don't like to have anyone do my thinking for me. But that's a minor matter which has faded into insignificance now."

"So now what?" Brandon asked.

"So now," Selby said, "I'm going out to his house, get his son out of bed and accuse him of being a hit-and-run driver. I haven't a single bit of evidence except a wild hunch to back up my accusations. It's a bluff. I'm either going to make it stick, or I'm going to dig my political grave."

"What have you got to go on?" Brandon asked.

"Virtually nothing except a hunch and some evidence that's too vague to be worth anything."

Brandon took his foot off of the runningboard, walked slowly and deliberately over to his car, switched off the motor and headlights, pulled out the ignition key, put it in his pocket, walked around to the other side of Selby's car, opened the door, and said, "Move over, Sylvia. You can sit in the center. All right, Doug, let's go."

"You're not coming with me," Selby said.

The sheriff grinned. "Try and put me out."

"Okay, Doug," Sylvia Martin said gleefully, "let's go."

Selby hesitated. "You might just as well," Sylvia said, "because I can see he means business."

Sheriff Brandon chuckled. "You certainly do know your men, young lady."

Selby made a little gesture of surrender, sent the car through the gears, ran swiftly down Main Street. "Anything new?" he asked the sheriff.

"Not too much," Brandon said. "Just the same old seven and six. Otto Larkin has been gumshoeing around town, letting himself be drawn into conversation about the murder—you know, he's been very reluctant to speak about it, but he keeps hanging around in the public places, where people can question him. He very painfully tries to avoid the subject for a while, and then finally blurts out that he thinks the girls know more about it than they've told and that *he* thinks it was a big mistake to ever let them get out of town; the officers should have struck while the iron was hot. Of course, he explains that he ain't criticizing anyone; and then he moves away abruptly, as though he's afraid he's said too much. He goes for a block and stands on that corner, until someone else comes along. Then he puts on the show all over again."

Selby said grimly, "Some day he's going to leave himself wide open."

Brandon nodded. "He'd like to see Roper
back in office. There was a lot went on then that hasn't
come to light. Larkin was in clover."

Selby swung his car up the hill, where the more exclusive residences were situated. "I wish you'd keep out
of this, Rex."

"Nope, I'm sitting in," the sheriff announced.

"Well, we found out a few things," Selby reported.
"We found out that the hitch-hiker's Emil Watkins, all
right, that he's the San Diego carpenter, that his daughter was killed by a hit-and-run driver. The car answers
the description of that formerly owned by young Stapleton and which he was in such a hurry to sell for a fraction of its price, and Sam Roper's representing the father
of Marcia's child."

"The devil he is!" Brandon exclaimed.

"That's right," Selby said. "There's a letter from a
firm of Chicago lawyers saying they've received a letter
from Roper."

"Any idea who it was?" Brandon asked.

"No."

Brandon said, "That may account for a lot of things,
Doug. If Roper's representing someone who wants to
avoid notoriety . . . And those letters from Marcia to
Watkins being published in the paper and all, Roper's
client must be pretty uneasy right now . . . and so's
Roper. . . . And that accounts for the way Otto Larkin's playing the game. . . . Hadn't you better let some
of this simmer before you tackle young Stapleton,
Doug?"

"No," Selby told him, "I want to strike while the
iron's hot."

"Well," Brandon said drily, "it's hot now."

"I wish you'd get out, Rex," Selby said, "and let me . . ."

"Try and put me out," the sheriff interrupted.

Selby turned the car to the right, shifted into second,
climbed for two steep blocks, and turned to the right
again. Rex Brandon surveyed the lighted house and said,
"They're evidently having some sort of a party in honor
of the old man's return."

"We'll crash the gate," Selby remarked.

"Want me to wait in the car?" Sylvia asked.

"You can take shorthand, can't you?" the sheriff inquired.

"And how!" she admitted.

"Okay," Brandon said, "you come in. Make yourself inconspicuous. When the going gets rough, pull out a pencil and paper and take shorthand notes of anything that's said. Pay particular attention to anything young Stapleton says."

"Don't worry," she assured him, "if he confesses I'll have it down in black and white."

Selby parked the car. The trio walked to the door and rang the bell. A butler answered the ring. "Mr. George Stapleton in?" Selby asked.

"Yes, sir. . . . It's the sheriff, isn't it?"·

"That's right," Brandon said, and, without waiting for an invitation, pushed past the butler and into a reception hall. The excited chatter of many voices came from a dining room in the rear. There was the sound of laughter, the noise made by silverware against glassware. "Where can we see him?" Brandon asked.

"In the Master's study, I guess, sir."

"All right, take us there."

The butler led the way through a library and into an alcove fitted up as a den, with a desk, bookcases, trophies, guns in a rack, and framed photographs on the walls. "If you'll wait here," he said, "I'll call him. His father has just returned from New York and is entertaining a few friends."

"So I noticed," Selby said.

Brandon stopped the man as he was about to leave the room. "Wait a minute," he said. "Don't tell anyone who's here. Simply tell George some people want to see him on a matter of important business. Don't tell anyone else anything. Do you understand?"

"Yes, sir."

"All right, go ahead."

Selby pulled his pipe from his pocket, grinned across at the sheriff and said, "Well, here goes."

Brandon resorted to brown cigarette paper and his cloth sack of tobacco. "All right, son, let 'er go."

They sat smoking in silence for a minute or so, then they heard quick steps crossing the library. The surprised figure of George Stapleton was framed in the doorway. "Why, good evening, Mr. Selby—Sheriff Brandon, and Miss Martin. Is there . . . did you . . . can I be of some assistance?"

"Come in," Selby said. "Sit down." Young Stapleton entered the room, hesitated for a moment, then sat down on the edge of a straight-backed chair. The stiffness of his posture showed that he was very much on guard.

"How long have you known Cuttings?" Selby asked.

"Why, we went to school together, and we were on the team together."

"You are quite friendly with him, aren't you?"

"Yes."

"You sold him an automobile, didn't you?"

"Yes."

"Didn't you sell it rather cheaply?"

"Well, perhaps I did. I was tired of it and I wanted to get a new one."

Selby, with a significant glance at the sheriff, said, "Stapleton, I have some bad news for you. We have every reason to believe that about the time you sold that car to Cuttings he went to San Diego, had a few more drinks than were good for him, and ran over a young woman. The woman died a couple of days later in a hospital. Cuttings never reported the accident. The car's been positively identified."

The room became strangely silent. The nervously rapid ticking of an ornamental mantel clock was plainly audible. Sylvia Martin, having surreptitiously extracted a pencil and paper from her purse, held the pencil poised. Sheriff Brandon, his face as expressionless as though it had been carved from teakwood, regarded young Stapleton with slitted eyes through a haze of cigarette smoke.

Stapleton gulped, started to say something, checked himself, bit his upper lip and said, "I can't believe that of Cuttings."

"Did Cuttings ever say anything to you about it?" Selby asked.

"No, he didn't."

"Let's see," Selby said. "Just when was it you sold him the car?"

"Why, I can't remember exactly when he took delivery of it," Stapleton said. "I might be able to look it up."

"When did you get your new car?"

"I can't remember that exactly."

Sylvia Martin said, "Perhaps I can help you there. I saw the new car right after Christmas. As I remember it, the dealer said he'd been trying to get it ready for Christmas delivery, but hadn't been able to because the order hadn't come in until a few days before Christmas."

Selby exclaimed, "Why, this accident took place on December eighteenth!" Once more there was a silence, while three pairs of accusing eyes stared at Stapleton.

Stapleton changed color. His eyes looked rapidly about the room, as though seeking some means of physical escape. He raised his eyes, to encounter the steady stare of Sheriff Brandon, and then abruptly lowered them. His shoulders drooped. A shadow fell across the room, as Charles DeWitt Stapleton's big shoulders framed themselves in the doorway. "What the hell's coming off here?" he demanded belligerently.

Sheriff Brandon said, "Good evening. We're asking your son about an automobile accident."

"What about it?" the man in the doorway demanded truculently.

Selby said, "Apparently his car figured in an accident. We were under the impression that it was after he'd sold it. Apparently he still owned it at that time. You must have sold it right afterwards, didn't you, George?"

"Don't answer that question!" his father said, and came striding into the room.

"Look here," he said, "I don't like this. I don't like the way you're handling it. I didn't like your attitude this afternoon and I don't like it now. What if my son *was* in an accident? He's insured. He's well able to pay.

What the hell are you trying to get at?"

"This accident," Brandon said evenly, "was a hit-and-run accident. A woman was struck down on the streets of San Diego. The driver of the car was intoxicated. The woman died two days later."

"When was this?" Stapleton asked.

"December eighteenth."

"And you're just getting around to pinning it on my boy?"

"We're not trying to pin anything on anyone," Selby said. "We're trying to get the facts, that's all."

"I know what you're trying to do," Stapleton said. "You're sore because I pointed out to you you were making a mistake in disregarding my wishes this afternoon. Now you're trying to go the limit and frame something on George."

"We're trying to find out the facts," Selby said. "George, were you driving that car in San Diego on the eighteenth?"

George glanced up at his father.

"Tell them you weren't," the older man said.

Stapleton said, "It's . . . there's a mistake somewhere . . . I wasn't driving the car. . . . I didn't hit anyone."

"Were you in San Diego on that day?"

"I . . . I can't remember."

"All right," Charles DeWitt Stapleton said, "that covers the situation. George has told you what he knows, and that settles it. He wasn't driving any car in San Diego under the influence of liquor. He didn't run into anyone. He didn't have any accident. . . . And get this, if there'd been any definite evidence connecting George or George's car with that accident, we'd have heard about it a long time ago. Coming at this late date, it sounds too much like a frame-up to suit me. What's more, I don't like the way you three were in here trying to browbeat a young boy. I think that covers the situation, and that's all there is to it."

"There are a couple more questions we want to ask," Selby said.

"What are they?"

"George, why did you sell that car of yours so hurriedly?"

"Because he was tired of it," the father answered. "I know all about that. George wanted a more modern car, one of the latest models. As a Stapleton, he has a position to maintain in this community. He doesn't like to drive obsolete, out-of-date cars, and I don't want him to, either."

"The car, I believe, was less than a year old," Selby said.

"There were new models out," Stapleton said, "and George liked the new models. My God, does my boy have to explain to the sheriff and the district attorney of this county every time he wants to buy a new automobile?"

Selby waited until young Stapleton's eyes met his. "George," he said, "isn't it true that you wanted to sell that automobile because you were afraid it might be traced to you?"

Charles DeWitt Stapleton interposed himself between Selby and the boy. "That question," he said, "has already been answered. I think we've covered all of the ground we need to cover, and I see no reason for prolonging the interview. As a matter of fact, George has been a lot more courteous and a lot more patient with you than I'd have been. If I'd have been here when you first came, I'd have told you to go to the devil. As it is, I want George to come with me and help entertain my guests. You'll excuse me and we'll excuse you. If you want to ask him any more questions, you can take the matter up with George's lawyer. Come on, George."

The young man rose, and the two started for the door.

Selby got to his feet, stood facing the older man. "Stapleton," he said, "you've seen fit to interpose your influence and your personality as a shield for this boy. I suppose you know what that means."

Stapleton, flushing, said, "You're damn right I know what it means! It means that I'm master of this house and that I'm finished being pushed around by an inexperienced district attorney and a comic-opera sheriff. It

means you two have bitten off more than you
can chew and you'll realize it before the week's out. Now
get the hell out of here."

Brandon started to say something, but Selby took his
arm. "Come on, Rex," he said.

The three of them left the house. Silently, they
climbed into Doug's car.

"Well," Sylvia said, "that's that."

"I'm sorry I got you into it, Rex," Selby said. He
started the car, kept it in low gear as he slid down the
hill on compression. He felt suddenly fatigued to the
point of exhaustion. The sheriff, fighting mad, said, "I'd
like to have had a show-down with him right there. We
could have put George in the car and taken him to jail
and questioned him there."

"It wouldn't have helped," Selby said. "He'd made up
his mind to brazen it out. With his father standing back
of him . . . and then again I may be all wet. That car
may not have figured in the case at all."

Selby realized that by tomorrow he would feel regrets.
Tonight he was simply too tired. All he wanted was an
opportunity to climb into bed and seek the oblivion of
sleep. He slowed the car for a boulevard stop, wearily
pushed in the gears and crossed Main Street. "Well,
Sheriff," he said, "I'll take you down to where you left
your car, and then we'll get a little shut-eye. Tomorrow
it may look different."

Sylvia said, "I'm afraid *I* won't sleep until I know
about the wicked coyote."

"What's this about the coyote?" Brandon asked.

Selby was too tired to answer. Sylvia told him, as Selby
drove the car. She finished just as Selby slid the car to a
stop in behind the sheriff's machine. "Okay, Rex," he
said, "I'll see you in the morning. Thanks for coming
along, but I'm sorry I let you do it."

"You couldn't have stopped me," Brandon said. . . .
"Say, Doug, I don't like this hostess's disappearance. I
was talking with a chap at the gasoline station who told
me he saw Triggs and Madge Trent driving uptown
around six o'clock this morning."

Selby, by a supreme effort, shook off his weariness. "Why, Triggs told me she wasn't out of the place," he said.

"Well, I don't think this boy was mistaken. He recognized the car and recognized both of the people in it. Now that makes it look as though she *was* the one who telephoned you from the All Night Drug Store. When you come right down to it, Doug, she had to be. She knew you were at the coroner's office. The two girls down at the auto court knew you were at the coroner's office. They're the only three who did. Of the three, this Trent girl is the one I'd pick as having put in the call."

Selby fought back his weariness. "Look here, Rex," he said, "we're going to be blocked at every turn here by Charles DeWitt Stapleton. He's going to be gunning for us, and he's going to resent any attempt to bring his boy's name into this affair. But there's one place where we could have a free hand."

"Where's that?" Brandon asked.

"Los Angeles," Selby said. "We would get the telephone company to give us the numbers Triggs called from the Palm Thatch. I have a hunch that every time some live prospect came in, Triggs telephoned this professional gambler he had on the string to come on up. We might be able to make an attack from that angle. This gambler, Handley, must know a lot about Triggs. If Triggs is mixed up in this thing we could make Handley talk, and . . ."

"Do you feel like going to Los Angeles right now?" Brandon asked.

Selby took a deep breath. Sylvia Martin said, "Doug and I will sleep on the back seat, Rex. You do the driving."

CHAPTER XVIII

THE LOS ANGELES sheriff's office was a bustle of activity. Cars roared up, backed into a parking position, with

their rear wheels against the curbing, ready to
dash away at a moment's notice. Drivers emerged from
the cars, slamming the car doors behind them, and hur-
ried into the offices. Various doors in the offices opened,
to disgorge people who dashed out to waiting cars and
tore madly away into the night. The chief deputy in
charge listened to Brandon's story, then pressed a button
and said, "Just a minute and we'll have a report."

Selby slumped in a chair, fighting to keep awake. The
warmth of the office, its stale air after the long drive
through the cold freshness of the frosty night, exerted a
hypnotic effect on him.

A man with the sallow complexion of one who has
been working nights, a green eyeshade across his forehead, a cigarette drooping dejectedly from his lips,
pushed open the door and stood in an attitude of silent
interrogation. The chief deputy said, "Here's a couple of
telephone numbers. Get all the dope on them. Also, take
a look through our files for a Carlo Handley. It may be
an alias. Dig into the *Modus Operandi* file and take a
look through the professional gamblers. Bring in any
photographs you find of a dark, slender, long-fingered
chap in the forties."

The man silently turned and left the room. The door
check slowly closed the door. The steam radiator hissed
comfortingly. Doug Selby's chin dropped forward. He
tried to pull his mind back from the black oblivion of
deep slumber, but subconsciously realized that the attempt was foredoomed to failure.

He awoke, to feel Brandon's hand on his shoulder.
"Okay, Doug," Brandon said, "we've struck pay dirt."

Selby looked at the photograph Brandon was holding
out to him. "That's the man," Selby said, his voice still
thick with sleep.

The deputy's voice showed interest. "This chap," he
said, tapping Handley's photograph, "is wanted. We've
been looking for him for some time. We've changed the
telephone numbers into addresses. The addresses don't
mean anything yet, but we're going to find out." He
picked up the telephone and said, "Send Steve Blake in

here if he's in. And have sledge hammers, riot guns, and a little tear gas ready." He slid the receiver back into place and explained to Sheriff Brandon, "You never can tell what you're getting into in these places. Sometimes they're on the up-and-up and sometimes you have your hands full."

Selby knuckled his eyes and yawned. He grinned and said, "I can't take it any more, I guess."

Sylvia Martin, her voice rich with sympathy, said, "Good heavens, you two have been up ever since three or four o'clock yesterday morning, tearing around at high speed. You've been driving steadily. It's a wonder to me you aren't dead."

"What you been doing?" the deputy asked.

Selby grinned and said, "Setting a trap for a coyote."

Before he could explain, a competent-looking individual, short-legged and broad-shouldered, stiff-armed the door of the office and looked inquiringly at the visitors.

"Steve Blake," the deputy introduced. "Steve knows how to handle these things. Steve, here's a card and finger-prints, also two addresses. This man's wanted, and wanted bad. Take four or five men and go places. This is the sheriff from Madison City, and this is Doug Selby, the district attorney. The girl's name I didn't get."

"Sylvia Martin," she said, "representing the Madison City *Clarion*, with a chance to pick up a little side money from the big agencies if anything breaks. So do your darnedest."

Steve Blake grinned. "You folks going along?" he asked.

"Are we!" Sylvia exclaimed, her eyes shining. "Try and keep me out!"

"Take two cars," the deputy said. "I've ordered sledge hammers, tear gas and riot guns; you pick the men you want."

"You boys know how these gamblers work?" Blake asked.

"To tell you the truth," Selby said, "I don't. I suppose, of course, this man Handley was standing in with Triggs. He probably gave Triggs a cut of whatever he won, and Triggs telephoned him whenever a game was going which looked promising."

"These birds don't work alone," Blake said. "They work in pairs, only you'd never pick the accomplice as being an accomplice. He looks like the biggest sucker of all. He's usually an open-handed, genial sort who pretends to be a rich retired business man who wants to play just for the excitement of it and doesn't care if he drops a wad of dough. He'll apparently be the prize sucker. The professional gambler will be laying for him. He won't be trimming any of the other boys in the game. But the fellow who's posing as the sucker will lose money to the gambler hand over fist. The gambler usually manages to tip off some of the other boys that if they'll play along to make the game seem on the up-and-up they won't lose anything. All the time it's the genial sport who's taking them to the cleaners. Then *he* loses *his* money to the crook."

Selby and Brandon exchanged glances. "Well, that's the way Handley worked it up in our county," Selby said. "A chap by the name of Morley Needham was nearly always in the game with him, and Needham was supposed to be a retired broker. . . . Shucks, I guess when it comes to knowing anything about crime, we just don't have the experience. . . ." He added with a reminiscent grin, "When you come right down to it, I guess we can't hold a candle to you city fellows."

"Forget it," Blake assured him. "You spotted Handley all right, didn't you, and brought us in the tip on him. He's been operating right under *our* noses down here and we never smelled a rat. Come on, folks, let's go places."

He led the way into an inner office where men were shoving shells into riot guns with the dexterity born of long practice. They had the completely impersonal attitude of people performing a routine duty. Steve Blake picked up a sledge hammer, dropped it into position over his shoulder and said, "On our way."

They followed him to the street and into two cars. Sheriff Brandon occupied the front seat of one of the cars, with Steve Blake doing the driving. Selby and Sylvia Martin sat in the rear seat. The motors throbbed to life, the cars sped away from the curb. Tires screamed as they rounded the corner with constantly accelerating speed. Under Blake's competent hands, the car slid through the late traffic. Selby caught his breath, but evidently the car wasn't going fast enough to suit Blake. He said, "Okay, folks, let's go," switched on a red spotlight, and kicked in with a siren. The car swung out, took the middle of the road and screamed into speed.

Selby had a kaleidoscopic glimpse of frozen traffic; late drivers who pulled into the curb, glancing apprehensively over their shoulders. They tore through boulevard stops, rocketed past an occasional street car. Street intersections whizzed by like telephone poles beside a railroad track.

Sylvia Martin clutched Selby's arm. "This," she said delightedly, "is the life!"

A street car had come to a stop to discharge passengers. Two automobiles had stopped behind it, blocking the road. The big police machine swayed over on its springs as it swung with undiminished speed out to the left side of the street car. Another street car was coming down the other track. The motorman gave one startled look at the glaring headlights. The blood-red beam of the spotlight fell full upon his face. He yanked the air-brake lever and reached for the bell cord. Steve Blake swung the car still farther to the left, siren screaming its imperative summons. An automobile following the other street car swung in close to the curb. The sheriff's car whizzed through the opening with inches to spare on either side. Selby let out his breath in a long-drawn exhalation. Blake, without so much as turning his head a fraction of an inch, said casually, "We run into things like that every once in a while. There's always a way through if you keep your head. Look behind and see if the other car is following."

Selby turned to look through the window. "All right," he said, "they're coming. They got through on the right-hand side."

"Street car must have started before they got there,"

Blake said. "We don't follow too closely. If the car in the lead *should* have a smash there's no sense in the other one plowing into it at sixty miles an hour. . . . All right, we're getting close. I'll shut off the siren and take it easy. No use giving them the alarm." He switched off the spotlight, and the car slowed to cruising speed. The second machine came up close behind them.

"Watch the numbers," Blake said to Rex Brandon.

Brandon lowered the window on his side of the car and pushed out his head. Blake switched on a spotlight which sent a brilliant beam of light playing over the fronts of the houses. "This is the sixty-nine hundred," Brandon said. Blake switched out the spotlight and said, "Three more blocks."

At twenty miles an hour, the cars seemed to be barely crawling. Selby felt that he could open the door, step to the pavement, and walk faster than the cars were traveling. He was tired, and he had been, frankly, frightened. The wild ride, in which cars dashed through traffic as though it didn't exist, had been too much of an unusual experience for him. But with the physical fatigue which gripped him, his mind saw things with the clarity of crystal. Significant bits of evidence clicked into place.

The car rounded a corner. The driver kicked out the clutch and gear lever, shut off the motor and coasted for almost a block. Then slid to a slow stop in front of a large residential building, a monument of somber respectability, its windows dark.

"Looks like we've drawn a blank," he said.

The other car came to a stop behind him. The deputies held a low-voiced conference. "Doesn't look so good, boys," Brandon admitted.

"I think we'd better try the other address," Steve Blake said. "After all, we haven't a great deal to go on."

They started the cars and turned the corner. Sylvia Martin yawned prodigiously. "Gosh, Doug," she said, "excitement is grand, but I *could* use just a little sleep."

Selby turned to say something to her. At something he saw, he suddenly stiffened to attention. "Wait a minute, boys," he said. "Look at all those cars parked in the vacant lot, and there in the alley."

Blake abruptly slammed on the brakes, cursed under his breath and said, "Serves me right for being such a sucker—and you were saying you country boys couldn't hold a candle to us." He opened the car door and said, "Come on, folks, let's go."

The other car found a place to park. Men, looking ominously purposeful in the darkness, spewed from it, to converge in a compact group which circled the residence.

Blake, Selby, Brandon, Syvlia Martin and a deputy climbed the porch, crossed to the front door. Blake pushed his finger against a button. From the interior of the house could be heard the jangling of a bell. Nothing happened. The little group, listening with strained ears, could hear no sound of approaching footsteps. Blake rang again. Abruptly, without warning, and with no preliminary sound of approaching steps, a sliding panel moved back in the door. Behind the panel was complete darkness, with only the blurred oval of a man's face showing gray and indistinct.

The man's voice, well-modulated, sounding surprisingly close in the darkness, said, "What do you people want?"

Steve Blake said simply, "We want in."

"Who are you?"

"My name's Blake. I'm from the sheriff's office."

"From the sheriff's office!"

"That's what I said."

"You can't come in here."

"Who says I can't?"

"I do. Do you have a warrant?"

"I have a John Doe warrant and a sledge hammer. Are we coming in?" Blake asked.

"We don't recognize John Doe warrants here," the man said, and started to slide the partition shut.

Blake drew back the sledge hammer and said, "How about this?" For a moment the man hesitated, then the panel snapped shut. Blake crashed the sledge hammer against the knob of the door. The sound of his reverberating blow was a signal to the men in back.

The booming of their sledge hammers pounding on the back door awoke echoes from the sides of the dark houses in the neighborhood. Blake splintered the lock. The door still held, a bar holding it near the top. Blake smashed a panel, found the location of the bar and started pounding on that. From the inside of the house could be heard voices, running feet, the sound of a woman screaming. Blake methodically swung on the door. The hasp which held the bar in position ripped loose. The door shivered back. Blake led the way in.

Selby saw stairs looming ahead of him. The lower rooms seemed dark. Blake said to his deputy, "Keep the door," and started up. At the head of the stairs, in a small room, a group of women in evening gowns were huddled together. Selby heard the sound of hurrying feet, the hum of voices giving excited instructions. Blake ran down the hall, pushed open a door. A group of men in evening clothes turned to stare at him in startled consternation. They were engaged in throwing things down a long chute which opened from a concealed door in the wall. One of the men, holding a roulette wheel, hesitated a moment, then moved toward the chute. Blake said, "Hold it, buddy," and went forward in a rush. The man tried to push the roulette wheel to the chute. Blake's fist crashed on his jaw. "That'll be about all, boys," he said calmly as the man staggered back, blood oozing from his cut lips.

The roulette wheel had thudded to the floor. Blake walked over to the sliding partition in the wall, moved it back into place, and said, "Pretty clever. Where does the chute go? Down to the basement? Or into a vault?"

No one said anything. A door slammed farther down the corridor. There were hurrying steps. A man pushed into the room and said, "Look here, what's the meaning of this? This is a private residence! You can't . . ."

"Well, well, well," Blake interrupted, "if it isn't our old friend, Chicago Dick, going under the name of Carlo Handley, I understand. And how about that confidence game business? How about the bail bond you jumped in

San Francisco? And how about the man-slaughter charge in Illinois?"

Selby grinned at the dark-faced gambler. "Remember," he said, "I was willing to bet you even money you had a police record."

Handley stared at Selby with concentrated hatred. The door behind him framed the figure of Morley Needham. "Come on in," Sheriff Brandon said with a grin, "and join the crowd."

Needham recognized the men from Madison City. "Well," he said, "I see that we are indebted to our rustic friends for this delightful bit of entertainment."

Blake ran his hands rapidly over both gamblers, in search of weapons, and said, "Where's a telephone?"

"Down the corridor, in an office. What's the idea?"

"Just thought we'd drop in for a social visit," Blake said, leading the way down the corridor.

A florid, fleshy man, with pendulous lips, purplish cheeks, and glazed eyes, sat at a desk, trying to look unconcerned. He had been feeding papers into a fire which burned in the grate. Blake said cheerfully, "That'll be all of that."

The man sighed tremulously. "Look here," he said, "this can be fixed."

"What makes you think it can?" Blake asked.

Handley said, "It's a squawk from the sticks. Triggs is back of it. They're after Needham and me. The rest of it's just incidental."

The big man's face worked with emotion. "Damn you two," he said, "trying to play that small town stuff. I told you the guys from the cow counties were dangerous. You can get away with stuff in the city if you mind your own business. You can't pull that stuff in the sticks and get away with it. . . . Look here, these men have been in my employ. I don't know what they've done outside of the city. That's up to them. Now, how about talking a little turkey?"

"Did you know Handley had a police record?" Blake asked.

"No, I know very little concerning him."

Blake grinned. "Well, get your things to- gether," he said. "You're going down to the station house and you'll learn more,"

Handley turned quickly to Needham. "This," he said in a low, tense tone, "is a bluff. Remember to keep your trap closed and . . ."

Blake's hand swooped down on Handley's stiff collar. As his grip tightened, the collar collapsed into a wrinkled mass. Blake swung his arm in a half circle, and Handley went spinning and staggering, to crash against the wall. "Enough of that," Blake said.

Calmly competent, completely without excitement, he moved over to the telephone, dialed a number and said, "Okay, send a wagon. This is a joint. We're holding a bunch of people." He dropped the receiver back into place, smiled affably at the men and said, "I think it'll be a lot better if we don't have any conversation for a while."

CHAPTER XIX

SELBY, wide awake now, but with a feeling of tension across his forehead, sat in the sheriff's office and looked across the desk at the deputy in charge. Rex Brandon, tough as saddle leather, apparently feeling no ill effects from his long hours of activity, struck a match to a hand-rolled cigarette and glanced across at Selby. Sylvia Martin's face was drawn and white. Her eyes seemed large and unnaturally bright. But she kept her head gamely erect, her manner was alert, and the pencil in her hand was ready to take notes of anything which she felt would be of interest to *Clarion* readers. "Well," the dep- uty said, "there you are. Promissory notes signed by George Stapleton, amounting to around twenty thousand dollars, an agreement assigning his share of any inheri- tance he might receive from his dad . . . and that's all."

Selby said wearily, "I know that these men are holding out. They know something about Triggs and about that hostess."

"Well," the deputy said, "try and get them to admit it. We've put them in separate rooms and given 'em both barrels."

Selby stared thoughtfully at the end of Sheriff Brandon's cigarette, watched the smoke curling upward. "I think," he said, "I know what happened, but it's going to be a job getting proof."

"If you think there's a kidnaping mixed up in this," the deputy said, "I'm willing to go the limit. You know, we don't go in for beating 'em up in this office, but we can make things plenty tough for 'em."

"I don't think it's going to get us anywhere," Selby said. "We might try telling Needham that Handley has confessed."

"That stuff doesn't work any more," the deputy objected, shaking his head. "It was a good line once, but it's been pretty well played out. It works with the dumbbells, but it doesn't click with the smart boys."

"I don't think these men are smart," Brandon said; "I think they're just about half smart."

"Needham's the one to work on," the deputy said. "The other one's got a tougher shell. He's been in the water a little longer. He's a fifteen-minute egg, or I miss my guess. His record shows it. Now then, we need Handley in our business. He's wanted three or four places. As far as Needham is concerned, he seems to have a clear record. We'll probably uncover something on him later on, but the point is we don't have it now.

"Now then, if you chaps want to claim that he's responsible for some crime up in your county, he's your prisoner. I'll turn him over to you. You can take him and take the responsibility for him, and I don't give a damn what happens to him. The only thing is if you take him over, *take him up to your county*."

Selby's eyes narrowed in thought. "Look here," he said, "suppose we do that. Suppose we take him up with us. There's a phone there in the jail which has a trick receiver. When a call comes in, you can hear it all over the jail office. Now, we'll take Needham up there and start to work on him. At exactly twenty minutes past seven,

you call me up on the telephone. I'll have
Needham sitting near the telephone. You say over the
telephone exactly what I tell you to. Can you do
that?"

"I can if you put it in writing," the deputy said.

Selby said, "Lead me to a typewriter."

The deputy found him a typewriter in the outer office.
Sylvia Martin said, "Come on, Doug, you're tired. Let
me take it."

Selby shook his head. "This," he said, "is one of those
things I have to do myself. I have to work it out, and, if
you don't mind, Sylvia, I don't want anyone else to
know what's in it."

"Okay by me," she told him. "If I can help you, let
me know."

Selby nodded, fed paper into the typewriter and
started tapping the keys. For thirty minutes he worked,
writing intermittently, pausing to stare, frowning, into
space, then writing again. When he had finished, he took
the paper out of the machine, put it in an envelope,
sealed the envelope, and said to the deputy, "Don't open
this until just before you put in the telephone call, and
when you call, do your best to make it sound con-
vincing."

"I'm making a note to have that call go through right
on the dot," the deputy told him. "Anything else we can
do for you boys?"

"Not a thing. Thanks. Keep working on Handley."

"Oh, we'll keep working on him," the deputy said.
"I've got a couple of boys in there now shooting a steady
barrage of questions at him. He won't get any sleep for
quite a while yet, but he looks good for as long as we are.
The worst of hammering them on this question business
is that the more we question, the more they know we're
groping in the dark. That gives 'em courage to hold out."

"If what I think is the case," Selby said, "he's going to
bank pretty strongly on the fact that Needham can bail
himself out."

The deputy nodded. "I have an idea there'll be professional bondsmen in the case within another hour, so if

you want Needham you'd better take him along with you right now."

"He's going right now," Brandon said.

They walked down the corridor to a room at the far end. Brandon pushed open the door. Needham, looking rather weary, and just a trifle frightened, sat in a chair where a bright light illuminated his features. Two men sat back slightly in the shadows. "Am I bailed out?" Needham asked, as Brandon opened the door, then, as he squinted his eyes, to peer past the dazzling light and make out Brandon's form, his face showed disappointment.

"No, you're not being bailed out," Brandon said. "You're not going to be bailed out."

"That's what you say," Needham said. "You boys wanted to make a bet the other day. I'll make you a good bet now. I'll bet you ten to one that there's bail here for me within thirty minutes."

"It won't do you any good," Brandon told him, "because you're going back to Madison City with us. There won't be any bail there."

"What have you got against me in Madison City? Just that silly gambling charge. I'll have a bondsman waiting at the jail door up there," Needham said confidently.

"Uh huh," Selby told him, "but it happens we're arresting you on a charge of murder. Try and get bailed out for *that*. Hold out your wrists."

Needham's face showed utter consternation. "What kind of a frame-up is this?" he shouted. "You can't . . ."

Brandon grabbed his wrists, snapped handcuffs around them and said, "The hell we can't! Come on, Needham."

The gambler drew himself very erect, his lips clamped into a thin line. "All right," he said, "I know your game. You're trying to get me out of this jurisdiction, where you can hold me without bondsmen knowing where I am. Don't think you can get away with it, because Handley will tell them. This is a boob trick, but if you hicks want to try it, go ahead."

"Suits us," Selby said. "Let's go."

They found Brandon's automobile where he had

parked it at the curb. Selby put Sylvia Martin in the front seat, while he sat in back with the prisoner. All the way to Madison City, Needham maintained a tight-lipped silence.

When Selby found that it was doing no good to question him, he dozed off fitfully, snatching what sleep he could. He wanted to relieve Brandon at the wheel, but the sheriff only laughed at him. "Shucks," he said, "I'm good for forty-eight hours more. The trouble with you, Doug, is that you're still young. You haven't toughened up. You're like jelly in the ice box which hasn't quite come to a jell. You need about thirty more years." And the sheriff chuckled.

"You," Sylvia Martin charged sleepily, "have been reading cook books."

"No," the sheriff said, "but I darned near got my ears boxed for raiding the refrigerator tonight."

It seemed to Selby to be weary ages that they drove through the cold night. He was thankful that the thermometer was not low enough to send a pall of smudge smoke down over the ground, but he was cold, cramped, and so mentally weary that his mind ached. Yet he felt that he had a solution of what had happened. It must be a solution. There was no other explanation. He realized that if his theory wasn't correct, he would be pilloried by a hostile press; that Charles DeWitt Stapleton would wage bitter and unrelenting warfare. He'd be laughed out of office. He was a gambler at heart—and he was staking his career on the turn of a card.

The car finally stopped in front of the jail. Brandon opened the door. The prisoner got out, looked at the building sneeringly and said, "I'll bet you don't keep me here for half an hour. I demand that I be allowed to telephone my attorney."

"Who's your attorney?" Selby asked.

"Sam Roper."

Brandon grinned. "What was it he said, Doug? I couldn't hear him. My right ear's a little bit stopped up. I guess I must have caught a cold."

"He wants to telephone a lawyer," Selby said.

"How's that?" Brandon asked, puckering his face as though making an effort at listening. "I can't hear you."

"I want to telephone my lawyer!" Needham shouted. "I demand that I be permitted to telephone him!"

"No good," Brandon observed with a tone of finality. "I just can't hear a word you say. Come on this way."

He led the handcuffed man up a flight of stairs. The night jailer opened the door and said, "Hello, Sheriff. What have you got?" The warm stench of stale air, heavy with the sweetish odor of jail disinfectant, assailed their nostrils. The barred door clanged shut with an air of finality.

"We're not booking him right now," Brandon said. "We're holding him on an open charge while we wait for developments."

"I demand that I be allowed to call my lawyer," Needham said.

"There's no reason for you to call a lawyer," Brandon told him. "You aren't under arrest."

"I'm not?"

"No."

"Then let me out of here."

"You can't get out without a clearance from the office," Brandon said.

"Say, what kind of a run-around is this?" Needham demanded indignantly.

Brandon looked at his watch. "Well, Doug," he said, "I guess we'll have time to cook up a little coffee and see if we can get thawed out. I guess you'd better sit right there in that chair, Needham, until we can get a clearance fixed up for you."

"You mean you're not going to hold me?"

"What grounds have we to hold you?" Brandon asked.

"Well, that's what I want to know. I demand that I be released."

"Sure, you'll be released," Brandon said. "The only thing is we have to fix up the clearance."

"Well, when are you going to fix that up?"

"There's a little red tape to be gone through with,"

Brandon told him. "Don't get impatient, and don't make so many demands. It's bad for your blood pressure."

They left Needham in the office with the jailer, retired to a little alcove under the stairs, where there was a gas plate and a pot of coffee simmering.

"Well," Brandon said, "we've still got five or ten minutes to wait."

Selby nodded. The hot coffee stung new life into his veins. "Lord," he said, "but I was tired. How about you, Sylvia?"

"I *could* use a little sleep," she admitted. . . . "This coffee certainly tastes good. . . . Tell me, Doug, what's your theory?"

"I don't know," Selby said, "but I figure these men must be mixed up in the disappearance of the hostess."

"How do you figure that?"

"Well," Selby said, "Rex Brandon went out there and accused her of having put in that telephone call, tipping me off that there'd been a murder committed. These two gamblers heard what he said. Now, if they had been the ones the hostess was going to warn me against . . ."

"I'm sorry I went out there now," Brandon said. "It seemed the right thing to do at the time."

"Forget it," Selby told him. "Anyway, you went out there and accused her of being the one to put in the call. Now, at that time, there were these two gamblers, Triggs and the hostess in the house. That was all. Now, Triggs knew that she'd put in the call, because he'd evidently gone uptown when she'd put it in. He may or may not have known whom she was calling. But, in any event, he knew she'd gone into the All Night Drug Store to put in a telephone call. Therefore, your charge wouldn't have surprised him very much. The fact that she didn't dare call from the place, but came uptown to put in the call, shows that she didn't want the call traced, in the first place, and in the second place, that she was probably afraid someone would hear what she was saying. She didn't want that heard. It all gets back to the fact that she was trying to conceal something from the gamblers. They heard you accuse her of having put in the telephone call. She denied it to you, but she knew she couldn't make the denial stick with the gamblers. So she had hysterics, ran up to her room and locked herself in. She did some thinking, and decided to slip out of the window."

"Well, what do you figure happened then?" Sylvia asked.

They heard steps on the cement corridor. The night jailer said, "There's a call from Los Angeles for Mr. Selby."

Selby looked at his watch, set down his coffee cup, said, "Come on," and sprinted for the office.

Needham sat by the desk in sullen silence. Selby picked up the telephone and said, "Hello, this is Selby talking."

The voice on the other end of the line sounded startlingly loud. It spilled words from the receiver and made them distinctly audible all over the office.

"This is Rockaway, the deputy sheriff in Los Angeles," the man's voice said. "We've been working on Handley ever since you left, and he's finally kicked through."

"He didn't look to me like one who would come through and tell the truth," Selby said skeptically. "I figured he'd sit tight. I thought our best chance was with the other one. What did he say?" Selby stole a quick glance at Needham. Needham seemed to be waiting for the glance. His face showed scornful disdain.

Selby cupped his hand over the transmitter and said excitedly to Brandon, "Handley has confessed."

Needham's laugh was sarcastic. "Why don't you birds try something new?" he asked. "This stunt only gets a play in the sticks. It's got whiskers."

Selby said into the telephone, "Give me the details, Rockaway, will you?"

"Well," Rockaway said, "we figured Handley the same way you did. He looked like a tough nut to crack, but it seems that he got to thinking things over and decided he wasn't going to take the rap for Needham. Here's what happened: young Stapleton was driving an automobile while he had a few too many under his belt. That was down in San Diego. He ran into a young woman and knocked her for a loop. He got in a panic and stepped on it and made a get-away. The young woman died. Her father was the hitch-hiker you found dead in the auto cabin.

"He talked with the daughter and got enough from her so he knew the section of the country the car came from, and got a pretty good description of the car. It was a distinctive sport job and he thought he'd recognize it if he saw it. He kept prowling around, up in the vicinity of Madison City, but didn't get anywhere until yesterday night, when he spotted the car parked in a shed at the Palm Thatch. He started crawling around the car, looking for evidences that it had hit someone, and getting the name from the registration certificate. He wasn't certain, because in the meantime Stapleton had sold the car and there was a new license number on it."

"Yes, yes," Selby said excitedly. "That all fits in. Go ahead and tell me the rest of it."

"Well, Handley and Needham came up from Los Angeles. Triggs had tipped them off that there were a couple of suckers at the Palm Thatch and it was a good chance to make a clean-up. Needham drove up first and caught some guy prowling around the automobile. He thought at first the hitch-hiker was trying to steal the car, so he put the screws on him. Well, in order to show them where he stood, he told Needham what he was after. He said his name was Watkins and that he'd identified the car as the one that struck his daughter, and was all excited. He wanted to telephone the police, and all that stuff.

"Now, of course, some of the details may be wrong here, because Handley is probably trying to protect himself, but here's what he claims happened: he and Needham both had a bunch of notes from young Stapleton. They knew that if Stapleton ever went to jail on a hit-and-run charge, the old man would clamp the lid down tight and those notes never would be paid. The only

chance they stood of getting their twenty
grand was to have Stapleton out where he could wheedle
the dough out of his dad. And even then it would probably take a period of time to do it. But they had an agreement by which Stapleton had pledged any inheritance he
might get, and they had plenty of plans for young Stapleton, and what was going to happen to his inheritance.
Now then, this is what made Handley talk: he says he
isn't going to be made a fall-guy in the thing. It seems
they knew Stapleton had sold the car, because they'd
been playing with him for a month or six weeks, and
knew it used to be Stapleton's car.

"Now, the way they've been playing the game, Needham was apparently the sucker. He'd always show up
first, and Handley would show up about half or three
quarters of an hour afterwards as though he'd been on
Needham's trail. So Needham, not knowing what else to
do, and wanting to wait for Handley, tied this guy up
and left him in the shed in this car. The hitch-hiker had
been planning to run the car in to the police, and he'd
had the motor started. Needham didn't shut off the
motor. He tied the guy up and left him in the shed.
Needham went into the Palm Thatch and killed time for
half an hour until Handley showed up. After Handley
showed up, he told him what had happened, and the two
of them sneaked out to the shed to talk with this man.
They found the exhaust from the automobile had filled
the shed with carbon monoxide gas and the man was
dead. Now then, that put them in an awful spot. They
decided they'd better call Stapleton out and tell him
about it, which they did.

"Stapleton had a bright idea. A couple of chaps by the
name of Cuttings and Gleason had a cabin they'd rented
down at the Keystone Auto Camp, but they weren't going to use it. They were on a weekend party with a couple of janes who had gone to bed, and these boys had a
cabin on their hands but they didn't want to go to bed.
They were making a night of it. They intended to get
some sleep later on aboard a yacht.

"Stapleton knew about this cabin. It was the only

place he knew of where they could ditch the
stiff and not have it appear he was connected with the
crowd at the Palm Thatch. They shut off the motor in
the car, dragged the stiff out of the shed, dumped him in
young Stapleton's car and rushed him up to the cabin.
Then was when Needham got a bright idea. Carbon monoxide poisoning is carbon monoxide poisoning no matter
where you find it. So he said, 'Why not have it appear
this stiff had crawled in the cabin and was waiting to kill
someone when the fumes from the gas stove overcame
him.' So they lit the gas stove, took the pencil from the
guy's pocket and penciled a note which made it appear
he'd been laying for someone with a gun. Needham had
a gun. They scrubbed the finger-prints off of it and stuck
it in the stiff's hand. Then they slid him in behind the
bureau and beat it. But they made one mistake. They
were pretty much excited and they wanted a good stiff
drink. Young Stapleton had a bottle of whiskey in the
glove compartment of his car. It was a bottle he'd short-
changed his dad out of on his dad's birthday celebration.
He also had some whiskey glasses in there. They poured
themselves stiff jolts of whiskey and then forgot and
left the whiskey bottle on the dresser when they moved
out.

"Now then, Handley says he doesn't want to be the
goat in the thing. He says he doesn't think it was an accident so far as Needham's concerned. He says Needham
deliberately turned on the motor in that car and left the
motor running for the twenty minutes or half hour which
was necessary to put this bird out of the way. He says he
can turn State's evidence and give you an iron-clad case
against Stapleton and Needham. He has a couple of bum
spots in his record so he's willing to take something of a
jolt, but he wants you to fix it up so all the sentences run
concurrently and he can go up from your county, on account of complicity in this murder business while his
time's running on these other things. But he wants to be
assured he'll get a light sentence. Then he . . ."

"He's a liar!" Needham yelled, trying to struggle to
his feet, and seeking to wrench his wrists from the hand-

cuffs. "He's a damn dirty liar! Turn State's evidence, hell! He's not going to turn State's evidence. He's the one that got me into it. I didn't want to. He dragged me along . . ." Selby gently slid the receiver back on its hook. Sylvia Martin's pencil was flying over the paper, taking notes in shorthand.

"Carlo Handley was the one who did the whole business," Needham shouted. "He came up half an hour after I did and found this guy with the motor running in Cutting's car. Carlo thought the bird was trying to steal the car, but the guy told him who he was and that that car had killed his daughter and he was going to take it up to the police. He'd managed to get it started by shorting the ignition switch. Young Stapleton had already told us about being sloshed and hitting a jane in San Diego. We were the ones who had advised him to sell the car where it'd be taken outside the county. Hell, we held Stapleton's notes for twenty grand. We *couldn't* let anything happen to him. Handley clipped this bird one under the ear and left him in the shed with the motor running. He joined us and we started to play. After half an hour, he went out and shut off the motor. Then he came in and told us he'd found this guy dead with the motor running. I knew right away what had happened, but I kept my trap shut. Stapleton swallowed it."

"All right, Needham," Selby said in a low voice, "go on and tell us about what happened after that."

Needham needed no urging. His face twisting nervously, eager words of accusation poured from his lips.

"If you want to know who really engineered the whole thing," he yelled, "go down to Handley's hide-out—a little bungalow out on South Figueroa Street! I'll give you the address. Look in the basement and you'll find Madge Trent, the hostess out at the Palm Thatch. We didn't know it at the time, but she followed Handley out when he went out to the garage to shut off the motor and pick up the body. She must have, because she put in a telephone call tipping you off. The sheriff spilled the beans, and she knew Handley was laying for her. She got out the window and got as far as the highway. Handley had doped out what she was going to do and he was waiting there for her and gave her a shot—Handley's a dope addict—I'm not. He gave her a big jolt. She went under, and we took her down to Los Angeles. Handley gave her another shot before we went on duty at the gambling place. He said that would keep her under until we decided what to do with her, but I knew what he was going to do—he was going to give her a big shot and plant her body in a cheap rooming house somewhere . . ."

Selby reached for the telephone. "What's that address?" he asked. "Come on, quick! Kick through with that address!"

CHAPTER XX

BY THE time Sylvia Martin had finished typing the confession, morning sunlight was sending a rosy splash of vivid color through the jail window. Selby said, "I want you to read that, Needham, and make certain it's correct. Then I want you to sign it, and I want you to put beneath your signature, in your own handwriting, that this is your free and voluntary confession; that it's made without any inducements or promises on my part; that you have not been threatened or coerced, and I don't want you to sign it unless every word of it is true."

"It's true enough, all right," Needham said. "It just shows what a damn fool a man is when he lets some other guy start playing his hand for him." He grabbed up a pen and started to sign the confession. Selby reached over, jerked the pen from the man's fingers, and said, "Read it."

Sylvia Martin dropped back in a chair, closed her eyes for a few moments. Rex Brandon, smoking one of his home-made cigarettes, watched Needham's face while the man read the confession. Selby, his nerves too tired to feel fatigue, having the peculiar feeling that his body was an automatic perpetual-motion machine which was func-

tioning independently of his mind, stuffed tobacco into the bowl of his pipe. The time was past when
he could snatch a few winks of sleep in between times.
Now he was too tired even for that. His body was
steeped in fatigue poisons. His nerves were taut as bow
strings. His pipe lit, he arose and paced the floor, taking
short, quick, nervous puffs at his pipe. Needham turned
the last page of the confession and said, "That's right.
That's exactly the way I said it. That's just the way it
happened."

Needham took the fountain pen and affixed his signature to the confession, then wrote under it a note to the
effect that it was his free and voluntary act.

"Now, let's get this straight," Selby said. "Young Stapleton didn't come out until after the man was dead?"

"That's right. I knew what had happened right away,
but young Stapleton never did know that Handley'd murdered him. Handley pretended that he'd just found the
body. You see, it would never have done for us to have
let Stapleton know that he could pin a murder rap on us.
You can't collect twenty thousand bucks from a man
who can send you to the gallows any time he wants to
open his mouth. We persuaded Stapleton that under the
circumstances the man had better be found somewhere
else, and he was the one who gave us the idea of putting
him in the cabin across from the two girls."

Selby glanced at the sheriff. "All right," Brandon said,
"let's go."

They took Needham back to a cell. Selby felt the
growth of stubble on his face and said, "I should shave
before we go up there, Brandon."

Brandon said, "I tell you what you do—come down to
my house. The wife will have some breakfast ready, you
two can take baths, and Doug can shave. How about it,
Sylvia, can I sell you on a nice hot bath?"

"And ham and eggs for breakfast?" she asked. Brandon nodded. She stretched her arms above her head and
sighed, then looked at her wrist watch and said anxiously,
"I wish we'd hear from the Los Angeles sheriff's office
on . . ."

The telephone rang. Selby grabbed up the receiver. In the silence of the jail office, the words spoken by the deputy in Los Angeles were plainly audible. "Say, Selby," he asked, "how about this? Do you know a guy by the name of Ross Blaine?"

"Yes," Selby said.

"How is he, on the square?"

"Yes. He's had a little trouble, but that's all fixed now. He's a good boy."

"Well," the deputy said, "all hell broke loose out there at the bungalow. This man, Blaine, seems to be in love with Madge Trent, the girl you're looking for. She tipped you off this morning on the telephone that a murder had been committed, but didn't have a chance to finish what she'd been saying. Something happened, and the guy who was driving the car got frightened and gave the alarm signal. She dropped the phone and sprinted for the car. Then she went back out to this road house and your sheriff came out there and accused her of having put in the call. The two men she was tipping you off on were where they could hear what the sheriff said. She knew that they'd kill her in a minute. So she dashed upstairs and pretended to have hysterics. It seems this chap, Triggs, was standing in with her. But he was even more anxious than she was that no one would ever suspect where the tip came from. She went to her room, slipped out the window and telephoned from a service station to have Ross Blaine come out for her. Blaine borrowed Stapleton's car and came down to join her, but she wasn't there. It seems Handley had beat the kid to it. He'd made her get in his car, shot her full of morphine, and drove right on down to the city. He must have started five or ten minutes before Blaine showed up.

"But when Blaine got into action, he got to going good. He figured out what must have happened, came down to Los Angeles and did some detective work on his own. He found out where Handley's place was and got in there. Handley had a mug out there acting as body-guard and keeping charge of things. He tried to carve Blaine up with a knife and Blaine got cut up pretty bad but the body-guard has a fractured skull and is still out. Blaine found the girl still groggy, and instead of reporting to us as he should, dragged her out to a hospital. Doctors have been working with her and have brought her around. She's out of danger now. But we had a devil of a time getting it all put together. She seems to be delirious. She's yelling for us to put through a telephone call and tell a girl named Ruby that the coyote couldn't dig out the mamma rabbit. I guess she's off her trolley."

"Are you at the hospital now?" Selby asked.

"Yes."

Selby said, "Okay. Go ahead and put through that call. It's on the level. Now get this: Needham has signed a written confession. The facts are just about as I worked them out in that statement I left with you in Los Angeles. We want to bring Handley up here on trial for first degree murder. What's more, we're going to make it stick."

The deputy said wholeheartedly, "If you can put a rope necktie around his neck, it isn't going to hurt my feelings any. He's been giving us the merry ha-ha ever since we started to question him."

"Well," Selby said, "about all you need to do is to tell him that you found Madge Trent and tell him where you found her and under what circumstances, and where the tip-off came from, and I think you'll find he loses his merry ha-ha pretty damn fast."

"On my way," the deputy said. "I'm going off duty now, but I'll explain all the circumstances to my relief so you can call the office and get co-operation. By the way, this Blaine chap and the hostess are going to beat it over to Yuma in Stapleton's car and get spliced. That is, young Blaine says they are. Is it okay by you?"

"Not only okay," Selby said, "but I'll buy 'em a wedding present. Give them my blessing."

The deputy said, "Don't you guys up in that county ever sleep?"

"No," Selby said. "We don't have anyone to come on for relief. We have to get our rest in between cases. Thanks for everything you boys have done."

"Okay," the deputy said, "glad to be of service. You're

the one who helped us out. That gambling raid netted some big fish. . . . Be good."

"I'll try," Selby promised, dropping the receiver onto the hook.

They went to Brandon's house. Mrs. Brandon, a motherly woman who had spent much of her life on cattle ranches and was accustomed to taking things as they come, broiled thick slices of ham, fried eggs and made hot-cakes. Selby shaved and bathed. The spell of unusual cold weather was over. The sun rode warmly in the heavens. The fronds of the palm trees in the sheriff's front yard cast deep black shadows on the lawn. Selby said, "Thanks a lot, Rex. I don't know just how to account for it, but I couldn't have gone to my apartment—not just yet, anyway. Somehow, I don't want to be left alone right now. I know we have a disagreeable duty ahead of us, and . . ."

"Same here," Sylvia Martin said. "My Lord! The thought of going up to my room to take a bath gave me the willies. Coming into a sane, normal home this way put my nerves back on par."

Brandon said grimly, "Well, it's no great pleasure to think of exploding a bombshell in the Stapleton house, but I don't mind telling you that it's going to do me a lot of good to watch Mr. High and Mighty Stapleton when he tries to bluff this thing out. Come on, let's go."

They drove up to Stapleton's house. Charles DeWitt Stapleton, in pajamas and bathrobe, had just come out to get the Sunday morning newspaper when they drove up. Stapleton's face darkened with rage as he saw them getting out of the car. "Now listen," he said, "this thing has gone far enough! I've had a long talk with George. He assures me there's absolutely nothing to it. You folks are working on a wrong lead and I want you to leave my boy alone. You're not coming in here."

Selby said, "I'm sorry, Mr. Stapleton. We have some bad news for you. I want you to believe me that you have my sincere sympathy."

"What are you talking about?" Stapleton asked.

"We want to see George," Selby said.

"I've just finished telling you that you can't see him."

"I think," Selby said, "that after we've talked with George for a few minutes you'll see things in an entirely different light, Mr. Stapleton. I'd like to give you every opportunity to minimize the publicity which is going to be inevitable."

"Publicity nothing!" Stapleton exploded. "You're the ones who are going to have the publicity. Wait until you see the roast you're going to get in tomorrow's *Blade*—a couple of hick cow-county officials feeling their oats! Why, you boys can't hold a candle to an ordinary city cop. You . . ."

Selby said evenly, "I'm not going to argue with you, Mr. Stapleton. You made that crack once before. I just want to tell you that since we've seen you, we've been practicing holding candles. In case you want to know it, we're going to arrest your son for murder."

"You mean to say you're going to claim it was murder because some goofey witness says he saw an automobile which resembled my son's . . . ?"

"No," Selby interrupted, "we're going to charge him with the murder of Emil Watkins, the man who was found dead yesterday morning in the Keystone Auto Camp."

Stapleton looked at him with wide eyes. "Good Lord!" he said. "You've gone *completely* crazy!"

George Stapleton, fully dressed and shaved, came to the door. "What's holding up the paper delivery, Dad?" he asked. "I want to see the sporting section and find out . . ." He paused abruptly as he saw the little group on the lawn.

Sheriff Brandon strode toward him and said, "Come on over here, George. We want to talk with you." Young Stapleton hesitated, half turned, as though he was intending to go back into the house, then reluctantly came toward the sheriff. Brandon said, "George Stapleton, I arrest you in the name of the law, as being an accessory after the fact to the murder of Emil Watkins, whose lifeless body was found in the Keystone Auto Camp yesterday."

Stapleton said, "You're crazy. My father's already told you just where you get off, and . . ."

"Your dad can fix up your traffic tickets for you," Selby said, "he can give you high-powered automobiles to chase around in, he can let you feel that you're superior to the law when it comes to the little things, but this time you've gone too far. You're facing a charge of first degree murder, George. If you want to come clean and tell the truth, and can prove that you didn't know Handley had deliberately left this man in the garage with the motor running, until he died from carbon monoxide poisoning, there's some chance we'll reduce the charge against you. If you sit tight, you're going up for first degree murder."

Stapleton's face twisted with conflicting emotions. There was a look of dazed incredulity in his eyes. "Handley locked him up," he said, "in the garage! And started the motor!"

"That's right," Selby said. "You see, George, they held twenty thousand dollars of your notes. They knew from talking with you why you'd sold the automobile. In fact, I think they were the ones who advised you to get rid of the car. Then, when the girl's father showed up, running down a slender clew, but one which was certain to bring results, they figured they had to get him out of the way if they were ever going to get that twenty thousand dollars."

Charles DeWitt Stapleton, seeming strangely undignified, and shorn of power in his baggy bathrobe, with his pajamas flapping about his slippered feet, said, "George, tell him he's a damn liar and come into the house!"

Young Stapleton, white to the lips, faced his dad and said, "He isn't a liar, Dad. He's telling the truth."

"What!" Stapleton asked.

George nodded. Brandon said, "Come on, George, you're going to have to come with us."

The older man stared at his son. "You mean . . . George . . . You didn't! . . . You couldn't! Damn it! Do you mean to tell me that you ran into some woman and fatally injured her and then ran off like a cad?"

"I'd been drinking at the time," George said by way of explanation.

"Been drinking!" Stapleton roared. "That's no excuse! That's only making things that much worse. What the devil did you mean?"

Brandon said, "That's a minor matter now. He participated as an accessory after the fact in a deliberate, cold-blooded murder."

"My son," Stapleton said, his eyes wide and staring.

"Your son—George Stapleton," Rex Brandon announced solemnly.

Stapleton's nerveless fingers let the rolled-up Sunday newspaper drop to the ground with a thud.

"You were rather free with your advice to us last night," Brandon went on. "I'm going to tell you something, Stapleton. In my days, boys didn't do these things, because their fathers put them to work pitching hay, doing chores on the farm and earning their education. It's men like you who are responsible for what's happening to the boys today. George was a good boy. You gave him a high-powered automobile. He got pinched for speeding. You bulldozed the traffic officers and got the tickets torn up. He was arrested once or twice for driving under the influence of intoxicating liquor. You fixed that up with your influence. Now then, try and fix this up. Come on, George."

Brandon took George Stapleton's elbow, led him toward the car. As they drove away Charles DeWitt Stapleton was still standing there in the center of the lawn, staring vacantly at the car which drove his son to jail. His face, puffy from sleep poisons, seemed to have aged ten years. His body had sagged down into his bathrobe.

CHAPTER XXI

SELBY opened the door of his apartment garage so that Sylvia could get her car out. He slipped his arm around her waist as they entered the half darkness of the garage. "Tired, Sylvia?" he asked.

"So tired," she said, "that I can taste being tired. . . . That's not all, Doug, I'm so proud I'm quivering all over."

"Proud?" he asked.

"Proud of you," she said.

"I didn't do anything in particular," he told her, "just plugged along."

"You *plugged* along!" she exclaimed. "You saw what must have happened, correlated all the facts and tricked those men into a confession. If that's plugging along I'd like to know what genius is. Brother, take it from me—some of the people in this town may not think you hold a candle to the big-city men, but . . . but . . . wait until you read *The Clarion* tomorrow morning, Doug Selby."

He laughed softly, held her more tightly to him and said, "Somehow, Sylvia, we seem to work together."

Her eyes, warm and dark brown, caressed his. For a moment she relaxed, then she pushed herself free. "Go away," she said, laughing nervously. "You make me feel too domestic, Doug Selby, and I haven't any time to feel domestic—not until . . . well, not until after I've written a story for *The Clarion* that's just going to knock their eyes out and bring a few tears to the surface."

"After that?" he asked. "Say tonight, about midnight —a little supper at the Palm Thatch?"

"Why the Palm Thatch, Doug?" she asked.

He said, "I want to have a talk with Triggs. After all, there's no reason why he should lose his license. He got too ambitious on the gambling, but in many ways you can't blame him for that. But . . . well, he drove Madge up to the telephone so she could tip me off that it was a murder. He knew those gamblers would kill both of them if they thought he was telling tales to the district attorney, yet, nevertheless, he did the best he could."

She twitched her lithe body in behind the steering wheel of the car with a quick motion, turned the ignition key and pressed her foot on the starter. "I'll see you tonight, Mr. District Attorney."

"Shortly before midnight, Miss Star Reporter," Selby said, bowing.

She nodded, smiled jauntily at him, backed the car out of the garage and into the street, snapped home the low gear, waved her hand and roared around the corner.

For a long moment Selby stood there in the sunlight.

His apartment seemed vague and unreal. His body was numbed into a weariness which demanded rest. But his physical fatigue could not dull his mind into repose. Dominating the tired muscles and taut nerves, his mind raced along with a smooth precision which enabled him to see things as though he had been looking through some mental telescope.

The telephone was ringing as he entered the apartment. He picked up the receiver and heard Sheriff Brandon's dry, emotionless voice making a report. "Just thought I'd let you know, Doug, before you got to sleep. Stapleton spilled everything he knew coming up in the car. I think he's on the square about the murder. He's good and frightened. On the hit-and-run business, he's hooked and knows it. It's been preying on his mind ever since it happened. Now then, here's something: he knows in a general way about Marcia Watkins. The chap who ran away with her is Hugo Larkin, the son of Otto Larkin, the chief of police. Personally, I don't think much of Hugo. He has a glib tongue and likes to use it. Evidently three or four of Hugo's friends in the younger set knew about Marcia—that is, they knew her by name. She was one of the girls who believed in a new order of things. Conventions didn't mean so much to her. Love meant everything, marriage nothing. Hugo played along with her and took advantage of her ideas. He probably loved her for a while. When he found the situation was serious and that Marcia was going to have a baby, he ducked out and left her to hold the bag."

Selby said, "I wonder if Otto Larkin knew that when we first found those letters."

"No one will ever know," Brandon said. "Larkin will deny it now, of course. But that's the low-down. Charles DeWitt Stapleton pulled on a coat and pants over his

pajamas and followed me up to jail. He's all
broken up. Honestly, Doug, I'm commencing to sympa-
thize with him. He realizes now how much of what happened was his fault. He wants to locate Marcia's child
and start an annuity for her to see that she has the best
care and education money can buy."

"Well," Selby said, "there's nothing we can do. That
hit-and-run business was in San Diego County. Stapleton's going to have to take his medicine down there."

"You're not going to proceed against him on the murder charge up here?"

"I don't think he's mixed up in it," Selby said. "I
think he fell for what Handley told him."

"Okay, Doug," Brandon said. "Thought I'd let you
know about Hugo Larkin and about Charles DeWitt
Stapleton's attitude. You'll find he's an entirely different
man when you see him. All the fight's gone out of him.
He's pretty much dazed."

"Thanks for letting me know, Rex. You'd better get
some sleep," Selby said.

"I'm going to—commencing right now," Brandon observed. "See you later, Doug."

Selby hung up the receiver, crossed his apartment to
the bathroom. The sight of his face in the mirror gave
him a distinctly unpleasant surprise. His skin was oily
and gray with fatigue. But he couldn't feel sleepy. He
wondered if he should have Doc Trueman give him a
sedative. He pulled his pipe from his pocket and sought
solace in it.

His doorbell rang. Selby opened the door. Inez Stapleton walked past him into the apartment. She had been
crying. Selby silently closed the door and turned to face
her. She met his eyes for a moment, then turned and
crossed to the window. She stood staring out into the sunlight. Watching her, Selby could see her shoulders square
with silent determination. She turned back to face him,
and her voice was steady. "Doug," she asked, "are you
big enough to be forgiving?"

Selby steeled himself. "Inez," he said, "I'm going to
do my duty. . . ."

"Oh, I don't mean *that*," she interrupted impatiently. "I mean with Dad, Doug. George is going to have to take his medicine. I don't know what it will be. I hope it isn't too bitter. But I hope it's bitter enough.

"George has been running wild. You know it and I know it. I didn't want to say anything when you asked me, because I thought it was a family matter and I thought it was up to Dad to clean it up. It isn't entirely George's fault. Dad's been too indulgent, and, above all, Dad's had an idea that his position here in the community made him not only bigger than the ordinary man, but bigger than the laws which governed ordinary men. He always felt that his wish should be law. I remember one time when an officer picked up George, driving while he was pretty well plastered. The officer brought him home. Dad was absolutely furious, not at George, but at the officer. Now then, that's come home to Dad and . . . and it's made an old man of him, Doug. After the sheriff drove off with George, Dad came into the house and jumped into some clothes. His hands were shaking so he could hardly dress.

"He was furious at you last night, Doug, and I was bitterly disappointed. I thought that you *could* have found some way of handling things so it wouldn't have been necessary to antagonize him. Now I see things differently. I think I understand something of your position, and . . . Doug, I just wanted you to know that I understand a lot of *my* position."

"Meaning what?" he asked.

"Meaning," she said, "what a darned unfortunate thing it is to have money. Look at me. I hang around this town, engaging in a round of social activities. If I went to a larger city I'd simply be swallowed in a larger round of social activities. If I went out and got a job somewhere I'd be taking wages which *I* didn't need, and depriving someone who did need the work of a chance to earn an honest livelihood.

"Please don't interrupt me, Doug," she said, as he moved toward her. "I came here to tell you things—to tell you about Dad and to tell you about me. I've been rotten spoiled. . . . I don't know, I guess I've been jealous. I've resented the fact that all of your time these days goes for other things, and I understand why now. I realize now that you're a worker. You have your life to live. You're interested not necessarily in a girl who works, but in a girl who has the type of mind which makes her *want* to work. I've . . . " She came close to him and put a hand on his arm. There was determination in her eyes. "I've called to tell you, Doug, that I'm leaving tomorrow to enter law school. I'm going to study law. I'm going to make something of myself. And . . . well, Mr. District Attorney, one of these days I'm going to be defending someone you'll be prosecuting and I'm going to make you respect *me*."

"Inez," he said, "please . . ."

She pushed past him to the door, jerked it open and turned in the doorway, chin up, eyes defiant. "I suppose," she said, "you have a date for tonight, haven't you?"

He sensed the desperation in her voice, knew something of the nerve strain under which she was laboring. He wished that he could find it in himself to lie, but he couldn't. He nodded.

"Go ahead," she said, "keep it. But remember this. From now on, I'm making something of *my* life. I know you, Doug Selby. You're going places. Not that you care about politics, not that you care about money. You're determined to make the most out of your life. . . . All right, I'm determined to make the most out of mine—I'll see you later."

"How much later?" Doug asked.

"When I get admitted to the bar," she said, and slammed the door.

Selby crossed the room, to stand where Inez Stapleton had stood at the window. He stood looking down at the street, saw Inez, without once looking back or up at his window, march across the strip of sidewalk, jump into the big cream-colored car and send it rocketing away from the curb. Selby raised the window. Warm Southern-California air poured into his nostrils. He dragged an easy chair up to the window, dropped into it. The sunlight bathed him with welcome warmth. To his ears came the first musical chimes of the church bells of Madison City, their notes mellowed and softened by the warm air of a semi-tropical winter day.

Slowly, the tension on Selby's nerves relaxed. Something which had been all wrong seemed to be all right now. He was too sleepy to analyze it. He dropped his pipe on an ash tray. A delicious sense of drowsiness enveloped him, his head nodded, dropped forward on his chest, and he slept.

〉〉〉 If you've enjoyed this book and would like to discover more great vintage crime and thriller titles, as well as the most exciting crime and thriller authors writing today, visit: 〉〉〉

The Murder Room
Where Criminal Minds Meet

themurderroom.com